Twilight

Also by Katherine Mosby

The Season of Lillian Dawes
Private Altars
The Book of Uncommon Prayer (Poetry)

Twilight

A NOVEL

Katherine Mosby

HarperCollins*Publishers*

HarperCollins books may be purchased for educational, business, or sales promotional use. For information, please write: Special Markets Department, HarperCollins Publishers, 10 East 53rd Street, New York, NY 10022.

FIRST EDITION

Designed by Joy O'Meara

Printed on acid-free paper

Library of Congress Cataloging-in-Publication Data
    Mosby, Katherine
        Twilight : a novel/Katherine Mosby—1st ed.
            p.   cm.
        ISBN 0-06-621271-5 (hc : alk. paper)
            1. Americans—France—Fiction. 2. Middle aged women—Fiction. 3. Paris
    PS3563.O88384T95 2005
    813'.54—dc22

05 06 07 08 09 ❖/RRD 10 9 8 7 6 5 4 3 2 1

For Bill Gaythwaite
and the friends
who stood by me
when it counted

Freedom is what you do
With what's been done to you.
—Jean-Paul Sartre

ONE

It would be misleading to say that the course of Lavinia's life was diverted by a kiss, or that a chance remark would change the continent on which she lived, although both things were true. Lavinia Gibbs was not known for being either sentimental or a helpless romantic. There was nothing helpless about Lavinia at all. She was, in fact, among the most practical members of her graduating class at Miss Dillwater's Academy, a trait much commented upon in her 1917 yearbook. Born at the turn of the century, Lavinia seemed always older than her years, but this was due to her reserve rather than her wisdom.

At boarding school, she had been told about a kiss the janitor's son had stolen from Maybel Skeffler, a senior who had excelled at archery until her feminine charms became so ample they impaired her ability to pull back a clean shot with the bow. All the girls had talked about the kiss in hushed tones, in the safety of the darkness, from their narrow cots, recounting Maybel's description long after she had been taken home. It had been a revelation that was disturbing and delightful in equal measure: the heat of his lips had made her swoon "down there." Afterward, even though the janitor's son was forbidden to set foot on the school grounds, just the sight of his father pushing a rake against a gravel path was enough to make Maybel Skeffler dizzy and liable to cry for no reason she could explain to her teachers.

Once, on a trip to Europe the summer Lavinia was thirteen, she had watched a couple embracing in a damp alleyway below the window of her hotel bathroom. It was the woman's moan that had caused Lavinia to hoist herself out of her bath and stand, dripping and soapy, on the closed lid of the toilet from which she could see, when she stood on her toes, the figures blending their bodies in the dank shadows that seemed to lick at them, swallowing now a chin or brow or shoulder.

By the time Miss Kaye, Lavinia's governess, knocked on the bathroom door, issuing directives about the attire Lavinia was expected to wear to dinner that evening, Lavinia had already been marked by the moment as surely as if she had been branded. Remembering the way the woman's voice had fluttered upward in the night, carrying a breathless urgency, Lavinia was flooded with enough jealousy and shame to make her ears burn.

That evening, before she joined her family in the hotel's rococo dining room, Lavinia spent an unusually long time examining herself in the standing mirror that filled a corner of the suite she was sharing with Miss Kaye. Lavinia had been told from time to time that she had beautiful eyes and lustrous hair, but the very fact that those two features had been singled out for comment signified to her that nothing else was worthy of praise.

Her mother had been a great beauty in her youth and even now, aged by unspecified "female" illnesses having to do with the birthing of her four children, Eliza Gibbs possessed an austere eminence that could still cause an appreciative murmur to sweep through a room when she entered, usually a little late and always impeccably attired.

Lavinia recognized in her own face the sharp, almost fierce, features of her father, a man whose distinguished career on Wall Street was only furthered by his passing resemblance to a peregrine falcon. It had given him an air of confidence that men respected and women found attractive in a vaguely primitive way; his was the face of a warrior and suggested a vitality and intelligence that were rarely questioned.

"Of my two girls," her mother was fond of saying, "you were given brains and Grace was given beauty and you should both be grateful for having been given any gifts at all, as there are plenty of girls who have neither. Besides, you are a Gibbs. Your name alone guarantees you a standing in society that most will never attain."

While those words were not comforting, Lavinia had enough horse sense to accept the truth they contained, even if it was bitter. Miss Kaye was more diplomatic: "A woman can do a great deal to commend herself to the opposite sex." Unfortunately, most of the young men Lavinia encountered at cotillions and debutante balls were less moved by the virtues of good posture, good manners, and good breeding than Miss Kaye supposed.

It was true that Lavinia was never a wallflower, the way Juliette Langhorn was, or Ruth Marshall, girls about whom unkind jokes were made by boys and girls alike, but if Lavinia was not at a loss for dance partners, it had as much to do with her sense of humor and her capacity to follow even the weakest lead as with her ability to be "alluring." Occasionally Miss Kaye allowed Lavinia to wear scent on her neck and would coil Lavinia's black hair in elaborate coiffures that showed it to advantage. Miss Kaye also had eyedrops from Germany that dilated the pupils, thereby highlighting Lavinia's best feature.

But the fellows who flirted with Lavinia never steered her across the dance floor to the balcony where, unchaperoned, they could importune her for a kiss. Her sister, Grace, older by two years, complained incessantly about forward boys and how she'd had to slap two different suitors. By Grace's eighteenth birthday she had rejected one proposal of marriage and was on the verge of accepting another.

Grace, moreover, was petite in stature, and before Lavinia had begun to menstruate she was already taller and more broad-shouldered than her older sister, a fact both her brothers teased her about with cruel delight. Ambrose, the eldest of the four children, the first son and father's favorite, called Lavinia "Mongo," which was the name of the African giraffe in the Central Park Zoo. Her younger brother, Gordon, the baby of the family and her mother's pet, called Lavinia "the vine" or when he was feeling particularly peevish, he would taunt her by chanting "four-story lavatory."

In addition to her concerns about her height, which made her feel ungainly despite her ability to move with surprising grace, she was also self-conscious about the fullness of her bust. Her mother and her sister were small-chested and, while it was never openly discussed, Lavinia was given the impression that there was something lewd about having large breasts, or at least unladylike. Mrs. Gibbs liked to disparage the laundress by saying she looked like a "wet nurse" or that Mrs. Brower's riding accident was because she was so top-heavy it affected her center of gravity. When Lavinia turned sixteen, Mrs. Gibbs told her not to take any sport at Miss Dillwater's Academy that required her to run, and before the holiday was over to have Miss Kaye take her to Lord & Taylor for a corset.

"And be sure to get one with bone stays throughout—not just at the waist," Mrs. Gibbs added. "You don't want to look blowsy or fast, if you know what I mean." In the photographs of naked women her brother Ambrose hid under the sheet music in the piano bench, only the very well endowed were represented, which embarrassed Lavinia almost as much as the discovery of her brother's secret stash.

The problem of her bust was only compounded by her height. Because she was tall for her age, if she were paired at dance class with a boy who was small for his age, his face was level with her chest. To avoid having a nose nestled in her cleavage, Lavinia would hunch her shoulders forward to a stoop just sufficient to protect her from the hot breath of blushing boys. Lavinia worried too that the consideration Miss Weingarten showed her during gymnasium at school was a sign that Lavinia's appeal was doomed to be appreciated only by the wrong gender, like a frequency too high or low to register with the average male.

It was therefore all the more surprising to Lavinia when her brother Ambrose's friend Jasper Perkins monopolized her at a cotillion honoring enlisted family members of the Knickerbocker Club. This was not only because he had earned a reputation at Yale for exploits with the "ladies" that couldn't be discussed among the "ladies," but because throughout the dinner she had watched her sister, Grace, flirt frantically with their brother's notorious blond friend.

They had known him from childhood; indeed, he had been the subject of many a cautionary comparison their father cited for his sons. Jasper's wildness had on two occasions required him to be taken home with a note the chauffeur delivered to his mother revoking Jasper's welcome in the Gibbs household for a period of six months. These exploits, of course, only made his company all the more desirable to the Gibbs boys and during those periods in which they were meant to be deprived of his malign influence, they simply met at his house, where the supervision was considerably more lax.

Lavinia had not forgotten the way Jasper had tormented her in the days she still cared about dolls by running them over with the Lionel train her brothers kept set up on the floor of the playroom. Jasper had never actually destroyed the dolls but they were nicked and scarred from his damaging games and general derision. "Jasper didn't have sisters" was the explanation Miss Kaye offered for his peculiar delight in making both the Gibbs girls cry before he lost interest in them entirely. It was from Jasper that Lavinia first heard the slang names for female anatomy, and it was Jasper too, who at twelve had appalled Miss Kaye by drawing nipples in red ink on a petticoat that had been hung to dry in the laundry room.

Not only was his attention at the cotillion unexpected, and therefore all the more significant to her, but Lavinia had never seen Jasper so combed and creased, and she was thrown off guard, allowing herself to see him as others did: handsome. Perhaps it was because he was attired in the white dress uniform of the Navy, his shoes polished to a mirror-like sheen she'd been told might reveal the undergarments of the girls who stood too close to their reflecting surface. Or perhaps it was because she could smell, under his lemony aftershave, a musky scent she would henceforth associate with masculinity. It may also have been the way Jasper cut in so smoothly before sweet, pudgy Herbert Burling had completed even one tour of the dance floor with her that made Lavinia so susceptible to Jasper's charm.

But it was not his charm that would haunt her later, when she compared the touch of other men to his. It was his unabashed sensuality, almost feral in its simplicity, that Lavinia found so compelling. First, he had gently moved her chin with his gloved finger, positioning her head so that her gaze was directed at his face instead of just to the right of his shoulder. Lavinia was unaccustomed to being regarded with such undisguised pleasure, and the boldness of his eyes had been disconcerting. Then Jasper pulled her firmly against him, not allowing her to create the cavity between their bodies that was her automatic protection against unwanted contact with boys.

She understood immediately when he pressed himself against her that he was aroused. "If you are trying to shock me," she said to him, continuing to hold his gaze as they moved together across the polished wood as smoothly as if skating, "you have failed."

"If you are trying to dazzle me," he replied, continuing to

maintain just enough pressure so that she could feel the way in which his body pointed at her like an insistent finger, "you have succeeded."

"I think you are confusing me with your other conquests. I may be inexperienced but I am not naïve." And with those words she broke off the eye contact that had bound them in an intimacy more alarming to her than the fact that she kept her thighs positioned to cradle him against her so closely she could feel him push against her pubic bone.

Jasper just laughed. "I didn't realize you had an ingénue's need for sugary words that melt on the tongue. I would have thought we could have used our tongues to more satisfying purpose." As he said this, he spun her flamboyantly in a double turn as they cornered the ballroom.

"Jasper Perkins," Lavinia said, "I've known you too long to ever play ingénue to your scoundrel." Returning her eyes to his, she added, "even if I wanted to."

"Rogue certainly and bounder is a given, but not scoundrel. I'm too well bred, and usually too well dressed." He lifted his eyebrows in mock beseechment and pushed himself more forcefully against her as they rounded the next corner and swept in wide exaggerated strides past the bandstand.

From across the room Lavinia could see Miss Kaye discreetly signaling to her. Miss Kaye, in her dowdy blue wool gown that never managed to shed the odor of mothballs no matter how much rosewater she sprinkled on the fabric before wearing it, was lifting her handkerchief in a tentative wave, like someone at an auction whose hesitation becomes increasingly expensive.

"If you don't like my attentions you have only to say a word," Jasper said to the curl sagging down her neck just behind her ear, despite Miss Kaye's efforts with a crimping iron.

For a moment Lavinia thought about lying, pretending she was offended by his arrogance and assumption. But, feeling his breath on her neck, she knew she was not enough of a hypocrite or actress to feign indignation, and besides, the truth was that she could feel the pull of a desire she had feared would always elude her, because she was a "lady," and not an especially beautiful one at that.

"I don't think it's your attentions I dislike," Lavinia said. "I think it's you. But I won't let that stop me from giving you a proper send-off."

With his hand on the small of her back, Jasper led her past the potted palms and the stone urns that flanked the terrace. Though Lavinia could never be sure how far she might have ventured, had not her mother's voice penetrated the night air like a sudden frost, it was a question that Lavinia revisited over and over. She never told anyone about their few moments alone, Jasper's outrageous behavior, and her full complicity in the kiss and the momentary caress of her thigh, keeping it even from Miss Kaye, from whom she had previously had no secrets.

Lavinia wondered whether Jasper had talked of it to her

brother Ambrose in a moment of bravado or camaraderie or sheer loneliness during their time together at the front, before Jasper was wounded and died of sepsis in a trench so muddy even his brilliant hair was dun-colored with dirt.

It was alternatingly a source of relief and indignation for Lavinia to realize that her brother would probably not have believed it, even if Jasper *had* revealed the brazen way she had responded to his brazen behavior. Lavinia wondered why she had not simply slapped Jasper at the outset, or, at the very least, stopped dancing with him at the end of the first waltz. Or, to be more accurate, she knew perfectly well why she had permitted him to do as he did and it worried her.

Lavinia feared her lack of umbrage revealed a character flaw from which she had been saved only because "some clumsy fool" had spilled wine on her mother's gown, prompting Mrs. Gibbs to end the evening abruptly. Mrs.Gibbs had gathered up her girls and Miss Kaye in such a rushed departure that Grace had to leave without her rabbit's fur muff because it could not readily be found in the recesses of the cloakroom.

On the way home, Grace had remarked sulkily that Jasper was certainly acting badly to have ignored the women at his table when common etiquette required him to see to it they all had an opportunity to dance.

"But Jasper has always been a bit of a barbarian and he was probably drunk or out to win some kind of bet. He's probably laughing about it even now, with Ambrose or Peter

Shiller," Grace concluded pointedly. Lavinia didn't reply, although the insult was not lost on her. Instead she smiled to herself in the shadow of the backseat, content to have made her sister jealous, and aware that the less she said about it, the more it would irk Grace.

Years later, Lavinia could remember with auditory exactitude the sound Jasper's chin made as it rasped against her ear, suggesting he had shaved too quickly and had missed a patch of stubble on the underside of his jaw. She could also summon to mind the trace of champagne and tobacco she had tasted on his lips when Jasper kissed her, and the shock of cold when one of his bright gold buttons grazed her skin.

In the years following the Great War, Lavinia was advised by her mother that the pool of suitable men had been so drastically depleted that Lavinia might have to consider a cripple or a Catholic for a mate. "You know, Lavinia," Mrs. Gibbs had counseled, "one can accustom oneself in youth to a certain amount of unpleasantness. Indeed, most marriages depend upon that ability. And the longer you wait, the more compromise you will have to accept, and the harder that will seem. Don't let yourself grow stale upon the shelf, my dear."

On other occasions, Mrs. Gibbs exhorted Lavinia to follow the example Grace set in marrying early and well. It did not reflect well on the family otherwise. Even Miss Kaye expressed concern in her oblique, solicitous way. "I personally washed all the linens in your hope chest with lemon juice and vinegar, my dear. I didn't want the lace to yellow. It never looks as nice once it has yellowed and then you'll have to use a caustic and that can be corrosive to the cotton fibers."

A few months before her twenty-seventh birthday, Mr. Gibbs took his daughter into his study one evening after dinner and closed the door. He took off his glasses and pinched the bridge of his nose, screwing up his face as if in anguish. After a long moment had elapsed in which Lavinia stood before his desk waiting to hear his admonishment, for a visit to his study with the door closed could mean nothing else, he finally burst out with "My God, are you determined to remain a spinster? Can't you even make an effort? Do you fancy yourself a pearl beyond price?"

His hand, Lavinia noticed, was trembling, and she watched him put it on the desk to steady himself during his outburst. For a moment, before she took the full force of his words to heart, she felt a pang of sorrow for him, a fleeting urge to put her hand on his to comfort him.

Then she felt the burn of tears begin to smart her eyes, and her throat constricted, making it impossible to reply even if she had had words with which to respond, and so she turned and left the room, without bothering to close the door behind her.

Years later in the back of her desk drawer Lavinia found the red leather diary that Grace had given her for a long passed birthday. The diary was almost pristine because Lavinia was embarrassed by the convention of addressing an object as an imaginary friend. As she thumbed the gilt-edged pages she found only a single entry.

"Dear Diary," she had written, "Why are unwanted suitors always the most persistent?" Lavinia tried to think back to the particular gentleman who had inspired her to sully the cream laid pages of her otherwise untouched book. It had probably been Edmund Parks, who was slight and nervous and licked his lips too frequently.

He had refused to walk barefoot on the beach on the one afternoon they had driven out to Coney Island. She remembered him capering alongside the surf in which she waded, his voice thin with concern, imploring her to come back to the boardwalk, his spats soiled by the wet sand, and his forehead sheening with sweat. When he had asked her if he could kiss her she had said no, a little too emphatically.

Even so, Edmund continued to call on Tuesdays and Thursdays for several more months, during which Lavinia gave him no encouragement whatsoever and yet he lingered like a tropical malaise. It was only the announcement of her engagement to Shelby Sterling that finally dissuaded Edmund from arriving with predictability twice a week, just as the hall clock was striking five, carrying flowers that always looked, like their bearer, slightly wilted.

There had been a few scrapes along the way with men Lavinia might have been able to love, or even fancied she did, but somehow their interest in her never ignited into anything more than a mere spark, just bright enough to illuminate the inadequacies of her other admirers.

There had been a young doctor at the Home for Unfortunate Women, where Lavinia volunteered three days a week, assisting the staff in the nursery. Despite Dr. Doyle's flirtation with Lavinia when she came to the infirmary, and despite the fact that he invariably sought her out in the cafeteria and had given her, for no particular occasion, a volume of stories by Washington Irving with woodcut illustrations, he had never called on her socially.

Dr. Doyle made her laugh and he frequently asked her

opinions about local politics and current events and sometimes asked her to read his poetry, and he stood very close to
her when she did. His poems were never about her, though.
They were always earnest descriptions of nature, often clichéd
and obvious but Lavinia found them stirring nonetheless.

Lavinia had also cherished a hope that one of her father's
junior partners, a fellow named Jonathan Wolsey, would take
an interest in her. She had been stunned by his verbal elegance, a gift that utterly eclipsed in her eyes his unfortunate
stoop and his discolored teeth. For a brief while, it appeared
as if he might reciprocate her interest. Then inexplicably his
visits waned and even his eloquence seemed to evaporate at
the few functions where periodically she would encounter him.

By the time Shelby Sterling asked for her hand, Lavinia
was thirty-five and she had long since abandoned any girlish
notions she might have had about being in love. There were
things about Shelby she found admirable; he had a sense of
fair play and honor, both of which were virtues she had come
to prize for their scarcity among the upstanding members of
her social set. He was tall; his manners were impeccable, and
she liked his voice, which was resonant and rich, and suggested a capacity for valor, or so she liked to think.

It was true that he interrupted her more often than he
should have and that he had a querulous side that was fatigu-
ing, but still she had grown deeply fond of his quirks. She
liked the way he laughed—there was such a sense of abandon
and delight that even when he was a tad too loud, she gener-

ously attributed it to his exuberance. Shelby read German poetry and collected glass paperweights and antique chess sets. He could be charming when the situation demanded and his hands were beautiful.

Sometimes, when circumstance allowed, he would take her unbeautiful hand in his and press it firmly. At first, that had seemed sufficient. It had been a relief to have a fiancé at last, and Lavinia was shocked to realize the extent to which her world now accorded her respect and welcome. On Shelby's arm she entered drawing rooms that had been inaccessible before or opened to her only for gala events at which it was understood that the unattached women who were long past being debutantes would earn their invitation by entertaining the dowagers and visiting family no one else would suffer.

With the ballast of a fiancé, Lavinia discovered her opinions had new weight at dinner parties and in the living rooms that lined Fifth Avenue. Finally, Lavinia was no longer relegated to being a spectator at social gatherings. Now her views were solicited even by the men who previously would have let her erudition and wit go unacknowledged rather than risk having its appreciation misconstrued. In her evening shoes, Lavinia was five feet seven inches tall, and confident enough to present herself as an equal. The attention she now garnered at dinner tables was not a source of pride for Shelby, however, but one of friction.

"I hope you won't let your need to opine overwhelm your understanding of what is becoming in a woman," Shelby said at the end of an evening at Justice Weston's house, as he adjusted his hat in the chill night air before offering Lavinia his arm. Lavinia noticed he did not have the courage to look at her while he delivered his injunction and, moreover, his left hand was clenched in an anger she could not fathom. From the side, his face was implacable and his pale skin seemed almost luminous with righteousness, though Lavinia knew it was really just the street lamp bestowing its glow on her betrothed.

Before he jammed his left hand in to the depths of his coat pocket, she saw his fist open and close in rapid succession, pumping like a small heart, and Lavinia had the queer feeling that she was seeing something secret, something essentially sordid in the way his beautiful hand fluttered involuntarily as if it were the only part of him sensitive enough to register emotion or disobedient enough to display it.

But Lavinia said nothing. She had, in the years she had spent in the company of her brothers and her father, accustomed herself to the capricious way in which words could be used like a lash on the most convenient target. Lavinia had learned that by presenting an impassive façade she could shield herself against the full force of the sting. If she concentrated elsewhere, she could limit the extent to which the insult penetrated the dark corners where it would remain like a virus, waiting to be activated by forces she couldn't control or predict.

Lavinia would often focus on some small flaw, a mole on

her father's neck, the chicken pox scar that marred Shelby's high forehead or the unattractive way his nostrils flared in anger, revealing more of the interior of his nose than anyone would want to see.

But if Lavinia distracted herself with the petty comfort of critical observations, she was also quick to recall the compensatory quirks and endearments that softened her impulse to distance and distain. She would recall the boyish way Shelby would pull on her earlobe when he felt affectionate, and the pet names he had for her which he would whisper when he held her, albeit awkwardly, in his arms, "Cricket" and "Mouse-cake" being the two he used most often.

There was no one to whom Lavinia could mention, even tentatively, the alarming and ironic truth of the situation: she occasionally felt greater loneliness in the presence of her betrothed than she did in his absence. Miss Kaye would have been the likely repository for that confidence but she had long since returned to Ireland. Miss Kaye had retired to keep company with a widowed sister and a nephew, a large-boned fellow about whose rabble-rousing Miss Kaye had sometimes expressed concern on the rare occasions she'd spoken of her relatives. It had been easy, during the years they had shared a home, for Lavinia to forget that Miss Kaye had a family of her own. Now, when Lavinia's need for Miss Kaye seemed at its greatest, she was dismayed to find herself jealous that she no longer had a claim, that she had been replaced in Miss Kaye's life by persons bound to her by blood.

It seemed to Lavinia a breach of loyalty to discuss the hollowness that filled her chest when Shelby discussed their future together, laying out before her, with the confidence of a general marshaling his men, the sweep of years that would take her to her dotage. Once Lavinia had broached the subject with her mother, who had looked at her blankly and then pretended not to have heard her daughter's question, as if the only polite response was to ignore it the same way the passing of gas in public would be strenuously unobserved. Grace, on the other hand, had laughed, and said dismissively, "You're just getting the jitters. Everyone gets them, though it probably is worse if you marry in your thirties. But look at your magnificent ring if you're nervous. An African-mined, round-cut, two-karat diamond should calm you."

It had never failed to amaze Lavinia that her sister, Grace, took such a devout interest in jewels. From the age of three, Grace had exhibited a precocious attraction to precious stones, often startling guests by asking to try on the rings and bracelets that her mother's friends wore to the house. By the age of seven, Grace cut pictures of jewelry from magazines and saved them in a wooden box she kept under her bed.

Only twice had Lavinia merited the privilege of being allowed to sit cross-legged by the footboard of Grace's bed for a viewing in which Grace spread across the counterpane all the photographs and drawings of famous gems, both set and unset, that represented her collection. As an adult, Grace knew arcane information regarding the provenance of certain gems, or with which family a famous brooch or prized tiara currently dwelled.

"You're right," Lavinia replied. "It's a lovely ring. And beauty is always a comfort," she added, taking her niece, Hadley, in her arms now that Grace had finished mummifying the baby in lace swaddling. Hadley was the fruit of despair: she followed four miscarriages and a stillbirth. Her conception occurred long after Grace had given up the hope of ever having a child.

Lavinia had not expected to have the baby thrust at her so abruptly, and it annoyed her. Momentarily, she wanted to squeeze the baby too tightly, as if to take from the daughter what she never could extract from the mother: the catharsis of tears, either the satisfaction of provoking them or the fulfillment of comforting them.

But instead, she leaned her face into the baby's until their noses touched, and she breathed in the chalky smell of milk the baby exuded, reminding Lavinia, with unexpected tenderness, of the nursery she had once shared with Miss Kaye. That was the end of Lavinia's attempt to discuss her concerns with her family.

Of the various explanations for her increasing discomfort at the prospect of her impending marriage, the notion that disturbed Lavinia the most was the thought that there was something wrong with her, something fundamental, something preventing her from claiming the happiness others found, and that now eluded her in the company of her betrothed. There was much to admire about Shelby Sterling, but the fact that Lavinia found herself having to anxiously catalogue his virtues at night, as she lay in her bed watching the shadows play across her ceiling, mitigated the reassurance the list might otherwise have provided. Moreover, the list she was reluctant to review, enumerating Shelby's failings and faults, seemed to swell with alarming alacrity.

She caught herself involuntarily wincing when she heard his voice booming up from the vestibule, announcing his presence as he handed the housemaid his hat, or when he cupped her elbow to steer her through a crowd, or when he told an anecdote she was required to appreciate. Sometimes she felt a rising panic she had previously known only in dreams, in which she was suffocating in a small space, or trying to run from a terrible danger but her legs were unaccountably disabled.

Shelby was oblivious to Lavinia's growing distress. When he let his arms linger around her shoulders as he helped her on with her coat, he mistook her stillness as feminine acquiescence, and when she busied herself with her gloves if he broached the subject of the honeymoon, he took it as an expression of virginal shyness. If at times Shelby found her accomplishments in the drawing room unseemly, verging on masculine, he took comfort in her modesty when he kissed her cheek and she looked surprised.

"Come here, Cricket," he would say, pulling her against his chest, and she would sigh and avert her eyes and he could almost forgive her for being taller than he would have liked, and more assertive.

"When we are married," Shelby liked to say, sometimes patting her hair reassuringly, "you'll see that I am right about this." It hardly mattered to Lavinia what subject he referred to: as confident as he was of her future enlightenment, Lavinia's doubts continued to deepen.

Shelby was treated by his mother to lavish attentions that seemed to Lavinia to border on the amorous. Mrs. Sterling treated Lavinia as if she were a rival who could not be openly attacked and had to be fought through subterfuge. Sunday luncheons at Mrs. Sterling's home were therefore long and taxing. Lavinia was embarrassed by Mrs. Sterling's effusively affectionate way of greeting her son, positioning herself in the doorway to embrace Shelby and simultaneously turning her back on Lavinia for an awkwardly long interval.

When at last Evelyn Sterling broke away from her theatrical reunion with her son long enough to acknowledge Lavinia, it was only to remind her of how lucky she was to have found Shelby, which Lavinia found decreasingly persuasive the more aggressively it was presented. Evelyn Sterling had another son but they were estranged; he had had the temerity to marry a woman who failed to pay homage at the domestic hearth over which Evelyn ruled. That son was rarely referred to by name after he moved with his wife to another city, a safe distance from Evelyn's capacious grasp.

Shelby, however, was happy to occupy the position of primacy in his mother's life now that she was a widow. He was flattered by his mother's coquettish fawning and basked in her admiration. Lavinia watched him relax and grow expansive as if only under his mother's adoring gaze was he able to be the man he aspired to being. His face would don a boyish eagerness that softened his features and caused the corners of his thin mouth to crinkle impishly and Lavinia would feel a tenderness that was easily mistaken for love. Nevertheless, it galled her that she was not the Penelope of his Odyssean epic; listening to the quotidian events of his day elevated to heroic stature, it was painfully evident that it was his mother to whom he unfailingly returned.

Evelyn was a smiling dragon of barbed innuendos, a vain and meddlesome woman with too little education or insight to be interesting, but too much self importance to relinquish control of conversation. Exacerbating these flaws in her personality was her inclination for alcohol. The prospect of consigning the rest of her life to the company of Evelyn made Lavinia reflect on her ability to forebear. Lavinia realized with surprising detachment how well she had been primed for the task, how her childhood experiences with two bullying brothers had taught her to withstand certain kinds of pain, while from the women of the house she had learned to shield herself against the sting of frostbite.

Evelyn sometimes went too far in her bibulous provocations and then she would make a solicitous gesture of recon-

ciliation which often included the gift of a bauble, a pair of
earrings she no longer wore, or a ring with a missing side
stone, something easy to part with. However, even these
tokens of friendship or apology were often revoked under one
pretext or another. Lavinia came to dread her generosity. Too
often it was a harbinger of a future insult greater than the one
the gift was meant to erase. Indian-giving, cheating at games
and breaking one's word were taboos Lavinia found particularly low. All breaches of trust were inconsistent with her
understanding of integrity, but those motivated by self-interest
and disguised as friendship were especially distasteful. It was
hard to even mention it to Shelby, but when she did, Shelby
defended his mother.

"Don't be so greedy, Cricket," he would scold. "They're
just things—the substance of materialism. Haven't you more
than enough already? You can't wear more than one bracelet
at a time, now can you?"

It was clear that Shelby did not wish to recognize that the
right to revoke makes the act of giving meaningless or worse,
offensive. But Lavinia was practical. She had learned the anodyne effects of discipline and distraction and, if those failed,
the refuge of resignation. During her long engagement to
Shelby, Lavinia became a dervish of activity, swelling her cal-
endar with luncheons and causes, appointments with the
seamstress and drawing classes at the Ladies League. She
read Gibbon and tried to learn Italian. She resumed the
piano lessons she'd abandoned as a young teen, only to con-

clude a second time, two decades later, that she had neither the gift nor the inclination to pursue an instrument. She taught herself to type and transcribed all of the letters her grandfather had sent home during the Civil War, collecting them for a privately printed edition she gave her father.

Lavinia joined a women's lecture series on Wednesday afternoons held in the basement of St. Thomas's Episcopal church, an institution she otherwise eschewed. But it was there in the back of the basement, at the end of the last row, separated from the rest of the audience by two empty rows, that Lavinia met Mavis Gelhardt.

The Gibbs family would have called Mavis a "trouble-maker" if they had ever had the chance to meet her, but Lavinia knew better than to let that happen. Mavis Gelhardt was a former suffragette who still wrote political tracts, dressed in men's flannel trousers, and smoked Turkish ciga-rettes openly, on the street, the way prostitutes did. Mavis was swarthy, with arresting blue eyes, and a strawberry mark on her brow she referred to as the kiss of the devil. Mavis had large, capable hands with which she hooked the most delicate lace doilies Lavinia had ever seen.

Often, after the lecture was over and the last question answered, the two of them would go out for conversation and coffee and sometimes a slice of pie. Mavis would take Lavinia to the Automat, where, amid the aluminum clatter and the steam of pressed humanity, she explained to Lavinia why it was her obligation as a woman to fight for her own happiness.

"Look," Mavis said, "think of it this way: no one else can. And besides," she added, "forget the moral imperative. Can you think of a better use of your time?"

When Lavinia tried to counter with arguments on behalf of altruism she was waved away by a fork or napkin or sandwich, whatever Mavis grasped in her hand at the time.

"But you enjoy the fight," Lavinia pointed out. "You seem to thrive on confrontation. Just think about how many ladies' clubs you've been asked to leave."

Mavis liked to say shocking things. She liked to watch the different ways her audience would respond with a bristle in the shoulder or a tightened jaw or their hands nervously busy with the search for something elusive in a handbag. Even among those who petitioned for women's rights, Mavis was considered too controversial to be included as a speaker at the meetings organized by her political colleagues.

"Masturbation should be mandatory for women until they learn to orgasm with the same facility as men," Mavis had pronounced at the Women's Philosophic League. At a rally for the International Ladies Garment Workers Union, Mavis had shouted out slogans so crude Lavinia hid behind a leaflet so that no one could see how aflame her cheeks and neck were. What had offended her, however, was not the message Mavis was imparting to the crowd but rather the coarseness of its expression.

Lavinia carried within her a secret and passionate love of words; an elegant phrase or beautifully turned sentence thrilled her in an almost visceral way. She was, therefore, especially intolerant of the clumsy or careless use of language. It was one thing to be merely prosaic, but to use words in a way that perverted their potential or denigrated their power was something that violated Lavinia's aesthetic principles. A particularly ugly coupling of words or leaden phrase could make her cringe, as if registering for the speaker the shame they ought to for speaking in such debased diction.

With Mavis, though, more than with the few girls from Miss Dillwater's Academy whose friendship she still found rewarding, Lavinia found herself able to confide for the first time without fear of judgment or gossip. It was the first time too that Lavinia had cause to consider and question her assumptions about the nature of friendship and to recalibrate accordingly .

"Your problem," Mavis diagnosed loudly, in an elevator ascending the Chrysler Building, "is that you are simply too philosophical about life."

Lavinia had tried to shush her, as she often did when Mavis became loud enough to attract the attention of strangers, but Mavis was undeterred by the discomfort of others. Embarrassment was a sign of repression she felt it her duty to expose.

"That's all well and good in school," she continued, ignoring Lavinia's distress, "but on the street it's a different matter. Unhappiness is a luxury you can't afford. If that's the bride price you have to pay to become Mrs. Shelby Sterling, I would say you are overpaying. You don't have to be a book-keeper like me to know a loss when you see it."

Despite injunctions and caveats from Mavis, Lavinia plodded forward with the preparations for the wedding, collecting pleasure where she could: in the selection of linens and a china pattern, the musical arrangement for the processional or the choice of bud for the ushers to wear in the buttonhole of their morning coats. She found, however, these moments of satisfaction were fleeting and ephemeral, like the breath exuded from an old atomizer in which the perfume has long vanished but its memory remains, or lines of poetry which rose from her unconscious as she fell asleep but disintegrated like smoke before she could write them down.

It was not until after Shelby finally kissed her with open lips that Lavinia finally understood she would have to break off her engagement. Throughout the preceding winter she had been troubled by Shelby's lack of ardor. Grace had teased her about how impatient Shelby must have been with such a long engagement, alluding to the lingering good night embraces in taxi cabs that had already reached their destination, or in unheated vestibules, or the furtive clutch in the parlor in a moment it was empty of others.

"Enjoy those tokens of thwarted passion," she had counseled Lavinia, "because they won't be repeated in marriage."

For months Lavinia assumed it was her own deficiencies that had dulled Shelby's desire. Twice she had changed her perfume and the colors of her wardrobe. She had included more daring necklines in the patterns she took to the seamstress and had had her hair styled in keeping with the leading ladies on Broadway. Shelby, however, didn't seem to notice.

Mavis had been blunt: "A regular guy will take what he can get. Something's not right." Mavis advised her to contrive a circumstance in which Shelby could not avoid the availability of her upturned mouth. "If you have to seduce your fiancé you probably shouldn't be marrying him. But if you are going to marry him, you really should know what kind of a kiss you can count on."

Lavinia might have found Shelby's kiss less objectionable if a series of small events had not burdened the moment with their cumulative weight. The day before the kiss, she had tried to buy a bag of roasted chestnuts from a vendor hawking his goods before the entrance to the park. Lavinia had avoided eye contact, as she usually did when dealing with merchants she did not know by name. It was nothing she did consciously; in fact, it would have dismayed her to recognize in herself some of the haughtiness with which her mother dealt so efficiently with tradesmen.

Her gaze noted that his jacket was stained on the sleeve and there was dirt under the nails of the hand proffering the brown bag of nuts. As Lavinia offered him the appropriate coinage to conclude their business, he closed her gloved hand with his. "No, Miss," he said, with a heavy accent she could

not place, "my gift to pretty lady." He had held her hand for
what seemed like too long a time. It was long enough for the
warmth gathered in his palm from warming it over the fire to
be transferred to hers, even through the cotton glove she
wore as a membrane protecting her from the world's touch.

Instantly, she snatched her hand away and looked at him
with more shock than indignation. He had very dark eyes and
a thick mustache and she dropped both the change and the
bag of chestnuts on the tray that separated them. As she hurried away she could hear him calling out to her, "Please, Miss.
Your change. Please, I make you gift." His voice had a pleading quality that was unfamiliar to her, carrying in its timbre
such eloquence that she lifted her gloved hand to her cheek
without thinking, as if the heat of his touch were still to be
found there.

She was several blocks away before her heart stopped
pounding in her ears and she was able to collect herself. It
would have been easy to dismiss the incident had she not
gone to visit her brother Gordon and his wife that evening.
Lavinia was not particularly close to any of her siblings,
although she continued to present herself at family occasions,
arriving dutifully with a gift in her hand for the niece or
nephew, and a determined smile for the adults. That evening,
while her brother Gordon was preparing cocktails and his
wife had repaired to her vanity to remove the lipstick left on
her cheek when they greeted at the door, Lavinia ventured
down the hallway leading to the farthest reaches of the apart-

ment, where the laundry, the maid's room and the nursery were sequestered.

The parquet flooring abruptly gave way to linoleum, dulling the crisp percussion of Lavinia's alligator pumps as she strode purposefully past the "public" rooms, to the quarters where the baseboard molding disappeared, and the walls waited to be repainted, as though the decorative impulse had so thoroughly spent itself in the living room and library and the rooms facing the park that there was nothing left with which to enliven the rooms withered from lack of light and a sooty view.

Lavinia was squatting awkwardly in her moiré cocktail dress, looking for an earring she had just heard fall when she felt a breath on the back of her neck and hands reaching into her hair. Lavinia shivered involuntarily and closed her eyes. When she opened them, she found Spencer, her five-year-old nephew, tilting her head back to see him standing behind her in rumpled blue flannel pajamas.

"Your hair is as soft as a rabbit," he said quietly, with a disconcerting earnestness, as if he had applied a poet's exacting consideration to all other comparisons before choosing this one as the most apt.

"Thank you, my dear," Lavinia replied, rising to her full height so that she towered over him like a giantess.

"I think that is the best compliment I've ever gotten from a fellow. Now show me your toys before I return to the adults," she commanded, offering him a hand by which to lead her. Lavinia was not fond of children generally because their innate capacity for cruelty and unchecked candor was usually a steep price to pay for their company. She was also aware of how a stinging nickname or sullen rejection could reverberate, echoing through a social world which occasionally deemed children and pets to be the secret dowsing rods for a collective discrimination.

Lavinia was therefore all the more surprised to find Gordon's young son had, with his one remark, touched her so deeply she felt tears well up and sting her eyelids. In the child's voice Lavinia had heard such a genuine expression of admiration she couldn't help but feel beautiful. As she paused to replace her earring and pat her hair before crossing the threshold back into the realm of parquet, she reflected on the fact that not once had Shelby ever said anything that had made her feel that particular pleasure, yet it was something a five-year-old had done with ease.

Then, on a cloudless afternoon after three days of rain, Lavinia had an argument with Mavis that had turned unaccountably bitter. They had spent the day together riding the ferry to the Statue of Liberty and back. Mavis had been horrified to learn that Lavinia had never descended into the nether world of the subway, or ridden on the Cyclone roller coaster or gone to a game at Ebbets Field. Immediately, Mavis had appointed herself docent and mandated a series of excursions.

It was on the way home, as they walked up Madison

Avenue that Mavis insisted, with an aggressiveness Lavinia found offensive, that Lavinia had made a Freudian slip and said, "Don't speak that way about my beloathed."

"Beloathed," Mavis repeated stridently. "Don't you hear yourself? You said beloathed instead of betrothed. How can you deny it?"

Mavis was shouting by the time Lavinia had crossed the street, walking as briskly as possible without breaking into a run. She held her arms crossed protectively in front of her and hunched her shoulders as if her back were registering, like armor, the strike of words Mavis spat across the street.

"You said it. I heard you say it, beloathed."

When Shelby came to pick her up that evening she was still feeling protective of him. She noted how striking he looked in his evening wear, and how he moved with an elegance that was effortless and enviable. He had brought her a wrist corsage of variegated ivy and sprigs of lily of the valley, and that, too, had pleased her. She had not expected anything and would have been happy with even the standard fare: rosebuds and pink ribbon.

As she emerged from the ladies' cloakroom at the Metropolitan Club, she felt a surge of elation at the notion that perhaps something as simple as a romantic kiss would break the barrier preventing her from loving Shelby the way she wanted, in requited ardor. After her first glass of champagne, Lavinia had persuaded herself that Shelby had only been waiting for a sign. He was just shy and old-fashioned, holding himself back out of respect until such time as she offered herself. He was too mature and dignified, she concluded, to paw a person without invitation, like the swains Grace used to complain of when they were girls.

At dinner, Lavinia could barely eat; instead she restlessly separated the corn from the succotash, lining the withered kernels up along the gold band that rimmed the plate's porcelain lip. She spoke little throughout the meal, even when Margaret Fogg was deliberately provocative, making inflammatory remarks about Roosevelt. Lavinia was too distracted by the sense of imminence that permeated the evening to be engaged by the conversation that wove around her. Without noticing it, Lavinia had absentmindedly buttered three dinner biscuits, before she realized they were noticeably crowding her plate. She managed to hide the rolls in her evening bag without losing the thread of the conversation Shelby had just commandeered to his end of the table. The butter would stain the satin lining of her evening bag, but she didn't care. It didn't matter that he had seated her at the far end of the table, next to a boring couple.

By the time the dancing started, Lavinia was suffused with a giddiness she hadn't felt since she was twelve, at Louise Buck's birthday party, when she'd won the relay race and her team had borne her across the lawn in a clamor of raucous excitement that was almost dizzying. During their first foxtrot Shelby held Lavinia more firmly than usual, and it had all the portents of an omen. When he asked her to recall the name of an acquaintance he had forgotten, Shelby had said, "It's an anapest and it's foreign. That's all I can remember about his name."

"Auguste Delaguerre," Lavinia replied, flattered by his assumption that she would know what he meant, as if he were speaking in a dialect that most people wouldn't follow but in which they shared a fluency. It attested, she felt certain, to an intimacy of mind.

Throughout their time on the dance floor, Shelby was charming. His observations struck her as clever and his humor, always dry as bootleg gin, had an added piquancy and spark. From the corner of her eye, she saw the swirl of other couples, the pale palette of taffeta and silk organza framed against the black background of men in tailcoats. She saw, too, the blur of women still seated at the tables who watched with longing, whose feet, she supposed, tapped out the rhythms of the band under the drape of tablecloth which hid them. For the first time that she could recall, Lavinia felt lucky.

As they left the dance floor, the band struck up a waltz, and she recognized it as the same Lehár tune to which she had danced with Jasper Perkins, years before, in her girlhood, when the world was still full of untested promise.

The kiss, therefore, when it finally happened, behind a Corinthian column, was all the more disappointing to her. She would never again see tongue in the butcher's shop without thinking of Shelby's kiss, and the way he had lodged his tongue in her throat and then left it there, motionless and flaccid until she thought she might choke. When she pulled away, she had to restrain herself from the powerful urge to wipe her mouth with the back of her evening glove.

In that instant, she knew she could not marry Shelby and she knew her family would consider her breaking off the engagement unforgivable. In the ladies' room to which Lavinia had retreated, breaking away from Shelby's embrace with such force that he inquired with concern, "Are you ill, Cricket?" she contemplated herself in the mirror, as if wanting to see herself as she was, one last time, before she changed her life irrevocably.

When the attendant, an elderly woman with a face made florid by years of drink, asked, "Shall I get you some smelling salts, Miss? You're looking a little peaked," Lavinia said firmly, "No thank you, that won't cure what's wrong, I'm afraid." Then she opened her evening bag and removed from her change purse enough coins to leave a small tower, precariously stacked, beside the three squashed dinner rolls on the cool marble top of the vanity.

From the upper deck of the *Queen Mary,* Lavinia leaned over the rail and watched her past recede. None of her family had come to see her off, though an expensive fruit basket had been sent to her stateroom as well as a few farewell bouquets. It had been suggested in certain circles that her family's letting her make the crossing unescorted was tantamount to disowning her. Lavinia knew better: the Gibbs family would never compound one scandal with another. She'd been given a modest income by her father; enough, he had said, to keep her out of trouble but not enough to attract it.

Her mother had given Lavinia the address of the best Episcopal church in Paris and the American Hospital at Neuilly, as well as some insignificant names at the American Embassy and the Consulate, but had not included a letter of introduction. Certain social contacts had deliberately been withheld from her, as if her expatriation alone would not sufficiently ostracize her. "They're all bores anyway," Grace had offered by way of consolation, and it was mostly true.

While the ship was leaving its berth Lavinia had waved to the well-wishers crowding the dock, calling out names and throwing streamers. It had seemed odd to be the only one at the rail not vigorously signaling to someone on land, and joining the boisterous activity of it made the departure seem a little less like an exile. When, however, her new green tam blew off her head and into the gray waters churned up by the ship's powerful engines, she decided it was time to go inside and unpack her toiletries.

Lavinia prided herself on being practical, and after she had had a loud, unattractive cry, she opened the complimentary bottle of champagne the purser had left in her room. While she drank a glass, she used some of the chips of ice from the silver bucket to make her eyes less puffy. Then, following a beauty tip Miss Kaye had imparted long ago, she dutifully held a sliver of ice against her upper lip until it was numb and slightly swollen. "Bee stung" was the way Miss Kaye had described the effect. "For those whose lips are on the stingy side."

Eliza Hatch and Dora Fell, friends from Miss Dillwater's Academy Lavinia had once asked to be her bridesmaids, had both sent carefully worded notes in which their wishes for a safe voyage barely concealed the somber tone of a condolence card. Mavis had sent a telegram with six words and no signature: "Good work, good luck, good-bye." Reading the message, so brief it had not even enough syllables to make a haiku, Lavinia realized how alone she now was. The force of it, the grief and fear, knocked the wind from her as though she had been struck on the chest.

Lavinia knew that Mavis would scoff at her weakness, decrying the need for companionship even while providing it. They had frequently discussed the handful of philosophers Mavis read at night in a rented room that sleep disdained to visit. Philosophy, Mavis contended, was the best cure for insomnia. "It brings you wisdom or it brings sleep. After two in the morning, either one will do. Besides, all the great minds have already done the hard work of the thinking for us. It's just sheer laziness not to bother to have a look-see."

It sometimes seemed to Lavinia as if Mavis had compressed all that she had learned into a single truth as hard and sharp as a diamond. "We are all alone and that's a fact. Everything else is just window-dressing." The first time Mavis had pronounced this, with irritating authority, was when Lavinia first inquired if Mavis had ever hoped to marry. The last time was at their parting.

"Those are the facts. Denying them or being a crybaby about it doesn't change them. It just wastes time," Mavis advised, clearly deriving a kind of solace from her severity. Lavinia, unfortunately, had never been able to take much comfort from the beliefs her friend had espoused in lieu of less reliable relationships. While Lavinia admired Mavis for the rigor with which she pared sentimentality from her life, Lavinia couldn't imagine comfortably inhabiting such a world for more than a few hours at a time. Mavis was fundamentally different from her: Mavis was unburdened by the concerns that lineage imposed. She had grown up in an orphanage; her actions reflected on no one and therefore excited no censure. She could smoke on the street, chew gum, and treat sex as if it were a sport that was more engaging with a partner but didn't require one. Her life, it seemed, needed no passion in life that politics couldn't provide. It gave Mavis a purpose and dignity not ordinarily ascribed to an unmarried bookkeeper living in a rooming house in Hell's Kitchen.

As she crushed the telegram into a small wad, Lavinia reflected on this irony: she would miss Shelby even more acutely than she would her tough-talking, suspenders-wearing pal who fancied herself a revolutionary. Despite the many things she'd found to admire about Mavis, Lavinia had never developed a closeness with Mavis equal to the one she'd had with Shelby. Now that Lavinia was freed from the obligation to be Shelby's wife, she found herself unexpectedly aggrieved to be without the particular charms and comforts Shelby had brought to her life. She had underestimated the depth of the bond she felt for him, regardless of her decision to forfeit almost all of the privilege she had known just to escape him. With Shelby she had forged an odd but powerful friendship, animated by shared intellectual interests and an uncanny, almost perfect accord aesthetically.

They had shared an eye, if not an embrace, and Lavinia was shrewd enough to know that the pleasure of seeing the world through the same prism of taste and expectation was more than just a pleasing convenience: it was a rare luxury she would not easily replace, given her exacting nature and the diverse and peculiar subjects that compelled her. She thought now with great tenderness of the way Shelby leaned on his vowels, giving his speech an idiosyncratic flair, as if he retained the traces of an accent from an unspecified else-where, more colorful and interesting than most origins, if only because it was imaginary.

Lavinia was haunted too by the memory of his wounded brown eyes when she had broken with him, blinking as if the impact of her words had temporarily blinded him. She was unaccustomed to thinking of him as vulnerable or defenseless and seeing his pain so perfectly exposed had been more ter-rible than she had expected. She found that when she least expected it, in the bath or crossing a street or stooping to straighten her stocking, she would recall some insignificant detail, like the brass dog tag he had saved from the collar of his first dog, named Kirby. Or that he kept it wrapped up in a handkerchief that had been his father's, stashed in a cigar box that still housed his skate key and three marbles all of which had some variation of cat's-eye design.

Lavinia would remember the way Shelby's quips had made her laugh and his erudite wit continued to amuse her even in recollection. A woman's red velvet cloche could suddenly conjure up the way Shelby would gallantly pluck the cherry from the top of her ice cream sundae, making a show of removing the one ingredient in the confection she disliked before it could stain the whipped cream on which it sat.

She remembered too, the way he would kiss her brow tenderly and say, "My darling Cricket," and "Good old girl," or even just "Sweet dreams, Mistress Mouse." Then, she would wince as if a barb had been wedged somewhere deep within her vital organs. Certain memories pierced like random arrows launched by nothing more than the sight of a commonplace object or simple phrase, or even the set of a man's shoulders when viewed from the back.

Lavinia wondered if what she felt for Shelby was what other people called love, and if she hadn't, like a fool from Aesop's fables, thrown *good enough* away in the name of the always elusive *something better*. Perhaps the passion for which she had so yearned was no more available to her than the whisper of genius or the gift of an angel's face or the ability to dissemble.

There were certain points in the day, like stations of the cross, when she was especially vulnerable to the lacerating pain these reflections invariably engendered. Often, it was at those moments when she was fatigued or lonely or taken off guard that she felt especially susceptible. She recalled Grace pointing to the spot on baby Hadley's skull that was not yet firm and the skin covering it was so thin a pulse throbbed visibly beneath the pale fuzz on Hadley's head. It had sickened

Lavinia to realize how delicate the infant was, not just because Grace had said, "You could poke your finger through if you're not careful," but because it was such a potent metaphor, so much more apt than the Achilles' heel, which had always struck her as too masculine and athletic an image to signify human vulnerability.

Finding her own carapace full of thin spots where sharp memories intruded, Lavinia had childishly hoped that she would no longer feel so porous among strangers, as if she could leave behind her on the diminishing shore all that had driven her from it. It hadn't occurred to Lavinia that, in fact, the radical privation of the familiar would make her cleave to it all the more. Even when she had been sent to camp in the Adirondacks, and Grace had pretended not to know her for most of the summer, Lavinia had not felt such a profound sense of aloneness.

From her handbag she withdrew a new lipstick, purchased specifically for the crossing. As Lavinia swiveled up the carmine column from its golden case she marveled at her audacity. She had decided that before she landed at Le Havre she would no longer be a virgin. Europe was no place to languish as a spinster; she could have done that in New England. Regardless of what happened to her heart, Lavinia wanted to know what it was like to let a man inside her. Her maidenhood was no longer something she needed to save; indeed, it was something she needed to spend.

Near the shuffleboard court, cocktails were being served

to the first-class passengers with upper-deck staterooms. A small band played earnestly, despite a saline wind that fingered their sheet music, and carried away the notes meant to encourage conviviality. Lavinia left after one flute of champagne and a labored conversation with a missionary couple en route to the French Congo. In the library, she secured two volumes of Trollope, a collection of Tennyson's verse, and a passenger list.

It seemed likely she would know a few of her fellow travelers at least peripherally, and she wanted to be prepared for whatever acknowledgments were necessary. The thought made her queasy and the alcohol disoriented her. As Lavinia made her way down a corridor she hoped would lead back to her stateroom, the ship rolled slightly. At cocktails there had been talk about the weather "picking up" but Lavinia had not paid much attention: weather was a refuge to which only the most bereft conversationalist would resort.

A heavy-set man in a blue cashmere blazer caught Lavinia by the waist as she stumbled and lost her balance, dropping her books and losing a shoe as she lurched forward into his welcoming arms. There was something about him, especially around his eyes, that reminded her of her brother Ambrose, making him seem familiar. She could see he was a little drunk, but so was she, so it only disposed her to like Eugene Turnbull more than she might have had they both been sober.

He kept his arm around her waist as he escorted her back

to her room and unlocked the door for her. He helped her into a side chair and put her books on the writing desk in a tidy pile. Eugene Turnbull's unctuous solicitude seemed like just the palliative Lavinia had been looking for, mitigating his other less attractive aspects. She wondered if he might be the material of her adventure. He kneeled before her, examining her ankle, holding her stocking foot in his hand and rotating it gently.

"It's not sprained," Eugene assured her, kneading the underside of her foot with his thumb. "My brother is a doctor so I know these things," he added, with a wink. Something in the wink repelled her, snatching her from the champagne stupor like a sharp whiff of smelling salts. Lavinia pulled her foot out of his hand and thanked him. She rose imperiously, despite the rolling of the ship beneath her, and ushered Eugene out of her stateroom and her life with one firm good-bye and handshake. If she wanted to, she realized, she could spend the entire trip in bed, reading, having trays brought to her. She could sleep and wake without regard to anyone's schedule. It gave her an odd feeling of weightlessness rather than the surge of elation she might have expected.

When night had fallen and she realized she couldn't see the shore and that even if she could, it was farther than anyone could swim, Lavinia was seized with panic. For an interminable moment she thought she was choking. It was probably in some measure to compensate for the helplessness she felt that she decided to steal one of the imposing green and gold tassels that punctuated like exclamation marks the lavish swags of silk brocade that draped her stateroom.

After she had laboriously cut the tassel from its gold cord with a pair of manicure scissors, she thought briefly of sending it to Shelby, for no better reason than that she imagined he would like it, but instead she tucked it into the toe well of a pair of walking shoes and didn't think about it again until she unpacked her trunk in Paris.

When she held it in her hand, in the unforgiving light of a southern exposure, it looked like a small animal she had killed. It was limp and severed and she was ashamed of herself. It was not an auspicious beginning.

Although Lavinia had been abroad only once before, her father had impressed upon his children the importance of having a quest when arriving in a new city. It gave the visit a shape and purpose which general sightseeing did not; it provided a goal for which the beautiful backdrop of a foreign city suddenly had a meaningful context as opposed to being a frivolous diversion.

Mr. Gibbs did not believe in pleasure for its own sake and he was suspicious of things that seemed too beautiful the way other men mistrusted what was easy. Lavinia had never understood it before; it had always seemed ungrateful not to embrace the pleasure of whatever beauty life threw your way, whether it was the Roman nose of a ticket collector or the crown of a cherry tree or a Chopin étude someone behind an open window was practicing.

In Paris, Lavinia found everywhere the kind of useless beauty that made her father nervous: in the variegated gleam of the cobblestones after a rain, or in the rust-colored moss that speckled the stone edifice of her hotel. It was giddying, and she could see why her father would have found the kind of surrender it prompted frightening, like being drugged, or crazy. It was true what Nora Fuller had said when she returned from her honeymoon—the light *was* different— more cadmium in the afternoon, and the morning light was so white it was almost blue. Or maybe it was the air that acted like a scrim through which everything seemed to shimmer and glow with an opiated sheen.

It therefore only increased Lavinia's delight to apply her father's principle and his money to a cause of which she knew he would not approve. Mr. Gibbs had often repeated an aphorism with such evident pride it was clear he was the author: "Women who smoke are like servants who drink: it is behavior that calls into question all previous behavior."

Lavinia may have failed to lose her virginity between continents, but she *had* taken up tobacco, and one of the first things she did after settling in to her hotel on the Left Bank was to acquire all the accessories of her new vice: ivory holder, gold lighter, and silver cigarette case. Lavinia watched, with an almost reverent attention, the way French shopgirls used cigarettes to gesticulate when they gathered like finches at the tiny round tables of cafés, and she made a point of imitating them. On the Rue Jacob, she bought herself an expensive notebook in which she began to keep a list of *Beautiful Things*, yet another project that would have galled her father, but ironically the one that led Lavinia to later discover her calling as a collector.

By the end of her first month, she had visited six museums and befriended a young nurse staying at the same hotel on her way back to England from Spain. Elsie Donner was freckled and plump and she laughed easily. She had lost Lavinia's Baedeker guide the first day she borrowed it and had returned to Lavinia instead a dog-eared *Guide to Cutaneous Infection and Dermal Trauma*. Tucked inside the flyleaf was a note explaining how the Baedeker had undergone a miraculous conversion at Our Lady of Notre Dame. The note concluded with the line, "But you can see for yourself how dramatic the change is. Even a skeptic would have to agree."

Lavinia might have been annoyed but instead the gesture delighted her. Elsie had managed to combine the ironic calculation and wicked pleasure that made her dimpled smile so disarming. Lavinia bought a new Baedeker's guide which she told Elsie had been the Kama Sutra before its visit to Saint-Germain des Prés.

"Go ahead and lose it," she dared Elsie. "I'm dying to see its next incarnation." That night Lavinia found in front of her door a copy of a book so smutty it had been left wrapped in newspaper, on which, written in lipstick was the message: *Shocking relapse!*

Elsie Donner's room was at the end of the hall, and didn't

include a private bath. Elsie thought nothing of wandering down the corridor to the communal claw-foot tub wearing only a Chinese dressing gown, through which the contours of her body were strikingly evident.

"What if someone were to see you?" Lavinia asked.

"Well, surely it wouldn't be the first time they were seeing the curves on a female body," Elsie said, dismissing Lavinia's concern.

"Besides, they'll never see it again, so why should I care? I'm only here for another ten days."

"But," Lavinia began in protest, when Elsie interrupted her. "And what they *really* want to see is this," Elsie added, exaggerating a wink as she flapped open the upper half of her dressing gown to reveal a flash of freckled breast, and then giggling, she ran back down the hall to her room.

Elsie and her brother had been among the first International Brigade volunteers in Spain. Her brother was there still. It was hard to reconcile Elsie's mischievous grin with a civil war but her fingernails were bitten to the quick and sometimes bled. She also drank in a way Lavinia had never seen a woman drink before: with determination. "I'll be right as rain when I get home," Elsie said. She laughed even about that, her being "all jangled up."

There was a sweetheart in Coventry she was going back to called Lanky Lou. She had known him since he was a choirboy. "But he's no choirboy now," Elsie always added, with the drumbeat timing of a burlesque. Even the first time, it had sounded rehearsed to Lavinia, and made her suspect, rightly, that Elsie was not the racy sophisticate she pretended to be. This was confirmed one evening when they were dining out at a café in Montmartre, with a Danish medic Elsie had worked with in Spain. While Sven was inside the restaurant paying the bill, a drunk had stumbled by their table and stopped to leer at Elsie. His attempt to flirt had been so slurred and foolish Lavinia had been amused but instead of dismissing his attentions as the tedious but inevitable price Elsie paid for her starlet allure, Miss Donner blushed to her eyebrows and burst into tears.

"I'm just overwrought," she said, drying her eyes with the napkin that had lined the bread basket. "I don't really give a sou about some old letch drooling in my direction. *Le salaud.*" It didn't surprise Lavinia, however, that Elsie knew the appropriate swear word and pronounced it correctly.

"You two go on without me," Elsie insisted. "I'm splurging on a taxi back to the hotel, my dearies, and Lavinia, don't expect to find any hot water left by the time you get back." As she waved from the window of the taxi, she called out raucously, "And whatever you do, don't get caught."

It was with Sven Larskan, in a borrowed apartment overlooking the Rue Monge, that Lavinia finally lost her virginity. "He's very brave," Elsie had said of him on their way to join him at the café. "My brother said if anything happened to him while we were in Spain I should turn to Sven. He can be counted on my brother said, and Bert trusts just about no one. Intellectuals least of all." Lavinia had never heard any-one described as brave before. The word alone was stirring. It suggested so much with just one syllable.

There was water damage on the wall of the apartment and patches of plaster had blistered and stood out in swollen relief, like a damp rash mapping the unexpected beauty of decay. In the amber light of dawn, it had a primitive power, like cave paintings, raw and delicate. Lavinia watched Sven as he slept, his mouth open and his arm flung wide in the famil-iar posture of a fallen warrior, like the figures that littered the foreground in the paintings of Rubens and Titian. The very twist of his torso conveyed an archetypical arrogance, as if even in sleep his body found its most flattering position, like water naturally finding its level.

His pale chest glowed against the white sheets, and Lavinia marveled at how young he looked, and innocent. Only his nipples, pursed in the cold air like a mouth express-ing displeasure, suggested a secret, angry energy that pulsed beneath his becalmed exterior. She was glad her encounter with him was unencumbered by the complexities of love; even the gulf of language seemed a useful boundary and she had felt relief and not frustration in the limitations it imposed on their conversation, grateful his English was rudimentary.

She could see how the temptation would be there other-wise to mouth the words of an ardor that was felt by neither of them, and she did not want to be confused or distracted by fictions she did not find necessary. Lavinia was much more interested in the deep pull that they had both felt when he had pushed her against the shuttered door of a newspaper kiosk and she let his hands translate the fundamentals of desire.

Her lower back ached and when she stood to stretch, a thin string of fluid leaked down her leg, sticky as egg white, but cloudy and streaked with blood. The bedclothes were smeared with blood too, but not as much as she'd feared. Grace had described her own deflowering as an event that ruined a perfectly good mattress. "It looked like we'd sacrificed a goat. It was gruesome. Thank God it was at a hotel and not on my fine linens." Lavinia wondered if she had bled so little because she had waited too long, like a fruit left to wither on the branch, desiccating with time.

Sven had not used a prophylactic. By the time he had found the right key on the unfamiliar key ring and coaxed the lock open with a combination of jiggling and cursing, he had forgotten about all other considerations besides getting their undergarments off.

It had made Lavinia laugh the way he had hopped around the small room, finally flopping on the bed, imprisoned by his pants and the shoes that obstructed his attempts to pull or kick them off. She imagined Shelby in contrast, proper, even dignified, bending to remove first his right sock and then his left. Thinking of Shelby sobered her and she left Sven thrashing his way to nakedness while she went into the bathroom.

She had wanted to urinate ever since they left the dance

hall; Lavinia had excused herself, but Sven had accompanied her to the lavatory and stood protectively outside the rickety door, waiting for her. "Too much riffraff," he said, pleased to use a slang expression, rolling the *r*'s with slurry pride. She had worried that Sven would hear her and, despite her need, she was unable to pee while he stood on the other side of the door, so close to her she could hear him humming drunkenly to the accordion music. The air smelled foul in the tiny cabin housing the hole over which she was expected to perch, and the footpads where she had positioned her feet were slippery from the back splash of the sluice bucket. She had decided to wait, and had left without relieving herself.

By the time she got to the WC in the apartment on the Rue Monge, it almost stung to release the scald of urine that stank of asparagus, and she no longer cared who heard. She didn't even bother to close the flimsy door that wouldn't have shut properly anyway. There was no point to being shy any longer—not once it became clear to her she was going to sleep with Sven.

He was brave and he thought she was handsome and womanly. Before she left, Elsie had told Lavinia in a rushed whisper that he'd used those very words. Sven seemed kind, and she liked the feel of his lips on hers. *He could be counted on.* At thirty-six, she was past any more conventional consid-erations than that. Lavinia smiled as she pulled her slip over-head and fell into the sag in the center of the bed. There was something solemn and symbolic about the moment, as if she were on the threshold of a higher world she could only know by bodily initiation. But she could also see the humor in the whole mad rush of it, like a *commedia buffa,* bumping over the stool by the entry and knocking the lamp to the floor and rolling around the bed like puppies. It was silly, almost slap-stick. "Go ahead and sleep with a man—whether or not you marry him," Mavis had advised her. "At least satisfy your curiosity, if nothing else."

Aweek after Elsie left Paris, Lavinia moved into an apartment on the Rue Bonaparte with a view of chimney pots on slate roofs from one window and from the other, the small graveled courtyard around which the Beaux Arts building wrapped itself with the grace of a sleeping cat. The apartment was more expensive than she had planned but she was close enough to the Seine to be able to smell the river after a storm, and the sharp cries of seagulls she never actually saw amplified the pleasure she took from having her own apartment.

Lavinia fell in love with its emptiness. When she moved in, there was only a dented metal bed frame and a wooden bookcase with badly warped shelves, but the high ceilings gave the two rooms a vastness beyond its actual size and the equally tall French windows lit the room with such brilliance in the afternoons that her rooms seemed more than full: they seemed sumptuous. She spent her first days in the apartment contemplating it from different points of view: crouching in a corner with her back to the wall, hugging her knees, or lying on the wood planked floor, looking up at the scarred beams that filled the uppermost space under the ceiling, like the rib cage of an ancient beast. Or she sat in the center of the room, cross-legged like a child or Indian chief, watching the smoke from her cigarettes twist and stretch into nothingness in the purifying shafts of light that pierced her room.

Lavinia did not invite Sven to the Rue Bonaparte, although she continued to see him well after Elsie left for England. They met at cafés or museums or Métro stations, depending on their plans. If they concluded an evening together it was in a cramped apartment on the Rue Daumier Sven was subletting from month to month until he could raise enough money to return to Spain with supplies and medical equipment as basic as stethoscopes. She was grateful that his presence in Paris was temporary. It limited the expectations that could reasonably be imposed on their union and gave camouflage to her ambivalence. Impermanence required discretion; it created distance to anticipate distance. It was one thing to be a free spirit in the world. It was another to bring it home.

She had been warned by Mrs. Beck, when she registered her new address with the Embassy, that her French neighbors might make her feel unwelcome; they were a nosy bunch, the French, scrutinizing every little thing, always ready with a criticism. Lavinia had no wish to court comment; indeed, she took refuge in the boundary propriety drew around her two rooms, making of her apartment a sanctuary only to be entered by someone worthy of sharing it. She was a Gibbs, after all, and believed in decorum.

Her concierge, a ruddy woman named Madame Luberon, had already begun a campaign of unaccountable rudeness. Whenever Lavinia pressed the brass button to release the outer door of the building and she stepped into the dank arched passage that led to the courtyard, but before she could get to the staircase coiled elegantly in the corner like a delicate metal spring, Lavinia could hear *"l'américaine"* spat like a poisonous slur from somewhere in the mildew and shadows.

By the time Lavinia's eyes had adjusted and she could discern from the gloom of the unlit passage the bulk of Madame Luberon, busying herself with some task that precluded eye contact, spitting into a rag to polish a hinge or sorting mail or sweeping a bucket of water over the cobblestones, it was too late for Lavinia to say anything other than "Bonjour" or "Bonne nuit." Lavinia was a private person by nature and she had no wish to parade even female visitors before the glass pane through which Madame Luberon guarded the building while boiling cabbage or tatting socks.

Moreover, after the hollow feeling in her chest had left, and the dull ache between her legs was no longer a reminder of how disappointing the act was for which she had so hugely sacrificed, she was embarrassed by Sven's gratitude, and the infatuation she did not return. Sven seemed, by comparison to the men she had known in the States, remarkably simple, which made it easy to be with him as long as he wasn't talking.

They went to inexpensive bistros, and there was a movie theatre near Montparnasse where they could get in for free because Sven knew the manager, and once he took her to an amateur production of a Molière play. On several Sundays they had gone browsing at the flea market at Clignancourt, and he had introduced her to his friends as they passed through Paris, but she was not really interested in legitimizing their sexual activities with the veneer of romance. She was unable to rekindle the same desire she'd had the first time Sven kissed her, and sometimes she was more interested in the way his nostrils flared when he touched her breast than in the sensation of his touch.

"Why won't you let me get to know you?" he asked her, when she shook off one of his questions about her family as spontaneously as if he had splashed her with dirty water. They were sitting side by side at a crowded café, their knees touching under the small round table. Her flinch jostled the table and set the two espresso cups rattling in their miniature saucers. Only that morning she had been to the Thomas Cook office near the Bois de Boulogne to pick up the stipend her father had sent for the next quarter.

Sven was staring at her, waiting. Neither of them touched the table to stop the vibration that filled the empty cups with white porcelain chatter. She looked down at his hands, which had tended the wounded in Seville and picked grapes in La Spezia. They were large and capable, scarred where he had knocked the tooth out of a sailor in a fight in Marseille, and where a fishing hook had gotten caught when he was a boy. All the kindness he had shown her was evident there, in his warm hands. For a moment, Lavinia imagined taking them in hers; she imagined accepting what he so earnestly offered, and letting it be enough.

Across the street, a cluster of schoolboys in navy blazers and short pants tried to push each other off the narrow side-walk into the street where pigeons darted fiercely at a soggy baguette in the gutter. Their laughter had the shrill edge of cruelty in it, heightening their hilarity, as though it were a necessary component in certain kinds of pleasure, swelling it like yeast.

Lavinia looked back at Sven. He would never fascinate her. It was unthinkable to say: being with him was as easy as treading water but no more engaging.

"How could you possibly know me?" she finally answered, her voice thick with finality and fatigue.

As they rose to leave the café, she watched Sven count out the change he was leaving on the table, his lips moving ever so slightly as he added up the coins. He had always been generous with waiters, although it was not required, and with drunks, especially those who littered the Rue Monge, waiting to collect the fallen fruit left in the street when the open-air market closed for the day. It was a terrible thing, he said, for a grown man to have to live like a dog.

A protectiveness welled in her as she imagined what her brothers would think of him. "Don't you see," she wanted to say, "it would never work. I was raised by wolves. It would only be a matter of time before I hurt you worse than this."

But Lavinia didn't speak: it seemed hopeless to explain. Instead, she reached down behind Sven's chair and picked his corduroy jacket up from the sawdust where it had fallen, and gently shook it clean.

When they parted in front of the entrance to the Métro station, they stood for a long time without speaking before Lavinia released his hand. She was grateful he was not making it more difficult.

"Thank you," she said.

"My pleasure," he replied, tousling her hair awkwardly in a gesture he had never used with her before. Then he descended the steep metal stairs into the station, taking them two at a time. The metal frame shuddered and rang with his tread like strikes on an anvil, and his departure echoed down the quiet street, amplifying his absence until somewhere overhead a voice shouted down from a window before banging it shut.

In the months that followed, Lavinia was stung by a loneliness she thought at times might be fatal. With the approach of winter, she realized how stark her days had become, how solitary and aimless. The false friendship of travelers, she had discovered, was ultimately too fleeting to be fulfilling, predicated as it was on a temporary displacement, and rarely surviving it. Moreover, those ephemeral connections were based on happenstance, which was not the best way to select companions, especially not if Lavinia's exacting standards were going to be applied. She had eschewed the lure of the expatriate community because she feared it would be familiar in all the wrong ways, replicating the limitations of the world she'd left without offering its salient compensations.

Lavinia found herself avoiding the Jardin des Plantes and

the corner parks, places where outcasts gathered. Even the silhouette of a solitary figure on a public bench could flood her with shame and sadness. Entire days passed without her having spoken and then when she did, buying a baguette or aubergine or a wedge of fresh butter from the blind woman who sat outside the pâtisserie, Lavinia's voice would be unaccountably high and thin, as if her throat had ossified from lack of use. She pounced on even the briefest exchange with a hunger that she could no longer dismiss as an effort to polish her schoolgirl's French.

As it became increasingly cold, and the moist breath of the Seine carried with it a chill that seeped into her bones on the long walks with which she filled her empty hours, Lavinia began to alter her routes. She found herself increasingly drawn to the Right Bank, where grand hotels lined the avenue and the air was rich with perfume and privilege. On the Rue de Rivoli, the shop windows lining the sandstone arcade displayed the opulent accessories of the life for which Lavinia was bred and from which she still found comfort, taking pleasure in examining luxuries she could no longer afford.

When she had first arrived, it had shocked Lavinia that in some neighborhoods the narrow streets twisting off the avenues in picturesque decay were rank with the astringent smell of urine. Twice in Sven's arrondissement, she had walked by men standing up against a wall, relieving themselves in full daylight. Magnificent monuments rose from streets with litter wedged randomly between cobblestones, like crooked teeth with food caught in between. It was not the juxtaposition of medieval and modern that was confusing to her; it was the unexpected ways in which splendor and squalor were married that was disorienting.

It was a relief, therefore, to sit on a brocade ottoman in an ornate lobby reading newspapers or just listening to English being spoken. She was particularly fond of the Hôtel Meurice, where the bellboys had the smartest uniforms, and the ashtrays were well distributed and frequently emptied. These outings became occasions for her to wear the couture of her class, the bias-cut silk dresses that flattered her lean frame, cashmere suits with fur trim at the collar and sleeves, gloves with pearl buttons at the wrist, finery she otherwise kept at the back of her recently acquired armoire.

She had stopped going to museums: the religious art depressed her. There was too much pain in the paintings. She was looking for comfort not censure and she found it in the gilded tearooms where wealthy travelers rested among their own kind. At first, Lavinia only ordered a pot of tea, usually a scented variety, Oolong or Earl Gray. She was not partial to the pastries powdered with confectioners' sugar or studded with candied violets, displayed in tiers on paper doilies like baubles in a jeweler's showcase. They were sweet in a fussy, unsatisfying way that reminded Lavinia of her sister Grace.

Even the pompous "Et voilà," with which they were presented, the gloved hand of the waiter stirring the air with a flourish somewhere between a bow and a blessing, and the final, solemn "Bon appétit," annoyed Lavinia. She was made uncomfortable, too, by the exaggerated deference with which her cigarettes were lit, or the chair pulled out from the table to seat her. It often seemed as if the assiduous politesse was thinly veiling a contempt only exacerbated by any effort to assuage it.

Lavinia discovered she could extend her stay by almost an hour if she included tea sandwiches in her afternoon ritual. If she skipped lunch first, it became her afternoon meal and thus provided a legitimacy to her loitering by giving it a definable purpose. The first time the tea sandwiches arrived Lavinia felt such a rush of emotion she couldn't eat. The delicate, crustless triangles, filled with watercress or smoked salmon or cucumber slices, reminded her of Sundays at Miss Dillwater's Academy.

She remembered how Virginia Hopkins used to pick out the cucumber slices, lick the mayonnaise off, and save them for later use on her eyes to make the dark circles disappear. Virginia never managed to banish her haunted look, but she later learned to used it to great advantage with college boys. Annie Ruggles, with whom Lavinia sang in the choir, would eat the sandwiches with tiny rabbit-like bites, starting first with the corners. Annie had died of influenza two months before they graduated, and her photograph had been hung in the chapel. Once, Lavinia and Eliza Hatch had tried to summon her ghost with the aid of a Ouija board until Dora

Fell got spooked and threatened to get Mrs. Thayer if they didn't stop.

Those friendships, burnished now by regret and distance, seemed more precious than Lavinia had supposed when they were readily available. It was true that Dora couldn't keep a secret, that she had a tendency to lie and an irritating laugh, and Eliza Hatch was competitive about even the most meaningless things, such as who finished brushing her teeth first or had longer hair or could hold her breath underwater for more laps. Even so, Lavinia found herself longing for their companionship whenever the plate of triangular sandwiches arrived.

She had written of course, sending at first souvenir postcards of vistas about which the usual exclamations of appreciation were made. She commented too on the fashions, "Even the police wear capes!" and the cheeses, "It might be impossible to try them all; there are hundreds of different kinds, including a few that smell like dirty socks." She did not mention the ways in which France seemed bitter, broken by a war from which, almost two decades later, it had yet to fully recover. It was not uncommon to see women who still wore black bands of mourning, reminders of how death touched nearly every family, spawning a virulent pacifism and accentuating a national xenophobia, expressed in *affiches* posted on walls and kiosks, graffiti written in chalk across sidewalks. Madame Luberon had lost a son at Verdun and a brother at the Somme and Lavinia's upstairs neighbor had lost her husband, and across the courtyard, Mademoiselle Breuille her fiancé and two brothers.

It was not uncommon to see sleeves or trouser legs pinned where limbs were missing, and now, veterans were having their pensions cut and unemployment was soaring. Lavinia knew that no one at home wanted to hear about the protests that spilled down the boulevards blocking traffic or that certain government offices were still waiting for telephone service. Not only were those topics outside the purview of her audience's interest, it felt wrong to expose the underbelly of her new city, like using the host's stationery to report the house's failings at the same time she enjoyed its hospitality.

When she could no longer adopt in her correspondence the breezy wonderment of a visitor, Lavinia had a die made with her new address and ordered engraved notepaper for the letters she wrote, filling sheafs of the crème-colored paper with innocuous news. The spring of 1937 was wet and unseasonably cold, she wrote, and everywhere she turned she could hear someone humming "Bei Mir Bist Du Schön." She did not write home about the constant strikes that threatened to delay the opening of the 1937 International Exhibition until 1938.

Lavinia omitted reference to what the newspapers called the "clash at Clichy" where the police shot into a crowd of unruly protesters, though she knew that Grace would have especially liked the theatricality of Prime Minister Léon Blum arriving at the scene in a tuxedo, having been plucked straight from the opera by his deputies. Observations were generally limited to what she could make amusing: the quaint racket of clogs on cobblestone as factory workers filled the streets at dawn, making alleys ring with their footsteps as if they were shod like the cart horses.

Lavinia described how a housekeeper had quit when she found a bottle of champagne chilling in an ice-filled bidet. "From the way she carried on," Lavinia wrote, "you'd have thought John the Baptist's head was in there on the ice." She did not write about the satisfaction she derived from polishing the silver herself or from buffing her leather boots to a high shine when she couldn't sleep at night, or that she sometimes ate raisins and chocolate for dinner or scrambled eggs with olives and mustard.

Most of the letters she wrote, however, never made it to the small postbox hanging like a metal rucksack from the wall of an adjacent building. Sometimes Lavinia carried them around with her in her handbag for weeks, until the envelopes were dog-eared and bent, soiled by flakes of tobacco that collected at the bottom of the silk lining, and by leaking fountain pens or the occasional skirmish with an uncapped lipstick or eyebrow pencil.

It would be wrong to imagine that the letters that did manage to get mailed went entirely without response. From Eliza, she had gotten a few short notes, filled with exclamation marks and pleasantries about how exciting life on the continent must be. Dora sent a cable inexplicably wishing her a happy birthday months before the event. Her sister Grace had written several letters, but they were mostly concerned with the upcoming auction of Madame de Monmarné jewelry. Grace was particularly agitated about a brooch which was said to have as its center stone a yellow diamond originally owned by Queen Alexandra in a different setting. Could discreet inquiries be made, Grace wanted to know.

There had been an overseas trunk call from Mrs. Gibbs informing Lavinia through an echo chamber that both delayed and multiplied each exchange, that Ambrose had made partner at his firm, Gordon's wife was recovering from a miscarriage but doing well, and Miss Kaye had succumbed to pneumonia.

"Of course we all miss you dearly," her mother added, "and I thought you'd want to know: Shelby is engaged to the Wilson girl. The one with the big teeth. Your father said not to tell you but I thought you should know."

The phone call ended badly. In closing, Mrs. Gibbs had tried to strike a maternal note, advising, "And whatever you do, don't eat the butter, darling. They don't wash their hands over there and the milk is not pasteurized."

"For God's sake, Mother, Louis Pasteur was French and besides, there is nothing to eat in this country that doesn't have butter in it," Lavinia snapped, the breadth of the Atlantic entitling her to express an impatience she wouldn't have dared at home.

"Oh dear," Mrs. Gibbs had fluttered on the other side of

the ocean, "now I've upset you. Your father was right—I
shouldn't have told you about Shelby."

The call had been upsetting but not for the reasons Mrs.
Gibbs supposed. Hearing her mother's voice for the first time
after so many months had unexpectedly brought to the surface emotions Lavinia had not acknowledged since childhood. She remembered how much she had loved watching
her mother dress for the opera, being allowed to select her
mother's evening bag or hair ornament. It was a task Lavinia
performed with the solemnity of an acolyte. She had known
her mother's closet by heart, not only because she liked to
hide there, behind the shimmery satins and the gauzy tulle,
amid the coupled shoes and paired boots lining the floor like
dancers in a processional, but also because Mrs. Gibbs's
dressmaker showed his appreciation for her large orders by
making the leftover scraps of fabric and trim into a wardrobe
for Lavinia's doll, Lilly, with the cracked porcelain face.

When Mrs. Gibbs was in a good humor, she would spray
Lavinia's neck with scent from the Venetian blown-glass
atomizer that crowned the collection of jarred unguents on
her dressing table. Lavinia remembered how exhilarating it
was, cold on her skin, like an icy whisper, its bouquet finding
a way into her flannel nightgown, and her pillow, released
anew every time she turned her head as she settled into sleep.

This memory recalled the cool of her mother's hand on
Lavinia's forehead, as if her mother's touch alone could put
out the fever that had sent Miss Kaye and the chauffeur out

in the Pierce-Arrow in the middle of the night to fetch the doctor. The whole of that illness, Lavinia had been allowed to wear her mother's pearl necklace, moving aside its loops of graduated strands for the doctor to place his stethoscope, which had the salutary effect of making Grace peevish with jealousy.

Suddenly, Lavinia understood that her mother too would die one day, and these memories would be all of her Lavinia had. The thought was searing, though not in the same way as the news of Miss Kaye's death. It had been Lavinia's plan to visit Miss Kaye in Ireland in the spring, and she had therefore not written to Miss Kaye with the incidentals of her new life because she had wanted to deliver them in person, in the safety of Miss Kaye's presence, the distinctly unsophisticated blend of baby powder and witch hazel that Miss Kaye exuded surrounding them protectively like a shield.

Although she was loath to acknowledge it, the fact of Shelby Sterling's impending nuptials stunned Lavinia with a more resounding sense of closure, and therefore loss, than the many difficult and shameful moments she endured in the breaking off of her engagement, precisely because now she was no longer involved. Her absence was complete; she had been replaced. She was fungible. She could return now.

Whatever damage she had done had been erased, whatever embarrassment she had occasioned would be forgotten as Shelby's life glided triumphantly on. Such was the nature of scandal; it was self-replenishing like the roll of waves along a shore, the next one arcing for its crash even before the last one had swept clear everything in its wake. She could return—but now she had no desire to.

After almost a week in bed, sleeping in her clothes and eating tinned sardines and potted fruit, whatever had accumulated in her kitchen that was not perishable, she arose galvanized by her grief. She thought of the line in *Coriolanus,* in which he embraces his banishment by pronouncing, "There is a world elsewhere." She would make of her life in Paris something more magnificent than would have been possible for her in the States. It would not be so hard after all, she realized, for she had never felt at home in the city of her youth. The great virtue of exile, whether imposed or chosen, was that it not only offered the possibility of a new beginning, it required it.

She began to take umbrage at the way the maître d' at the Crillon nodded his head gravely when he saw her, enunciating the word *mademoiselle*, so lingeringly that the four syllables sounded like an insult. Lavinia had previously contemplated buying a gold band to wear on the ring finger of her left hand but had never been able to bring herself to do it. Now she was glad of that. It had been her choice, after all, not to marry when she had the chance, and it now galled her to think that she had almost let a hotel employee intimidate her because she lacked the honorific without which women of her age were rendered inconsequential, particularly, she noted, by the less educated classes.

When Lavinia returned to the world, after a week of weeping in bed, and pacing the perimeter of her flat, it was because she longed for the sky and oysters and fresh bread and she could no longer stand to listen to Madame Luberon fill the courtyard with the reverberating argot she used to berate her husband, Lavinia's very first errand was to go to a jewelry store on the Avenue Saint-Honoré and make a purchase. Instead of disguising her unmarried state with a faux wedding ring, she flaunted it with the purchase of gold bangles to line her wrist so that every time she moved her left hand she drew attention to it with the brazen clatter of the bracelets.

Lavinia was sitting in one of the last pews at the church of Saint-Germain des Prés, listening to a concert of Bach's organ music, letting her mind drift when she had her revelation. Because she was not religious, she tended to regard those who were with either pity or disdain. Church had always been for her family more of a social than a spiritual event, and an occasion to sing. Faith, Lavinia felt, was a compensation for those without the intellectual rigor to question it.

A chill rose from the pocked stone floor of the church, and the musty smell of dampness competed with the dry scent of sandalwood and the tang of myrrh still lingering from the morning service. Lavinia had chosen to sit in a pew next to one of the painted columns rising up like the trunk of a tree linking this world with the heavenly realm, holding up the curve of arch where fading gold stars scattered across the indigo background, dulled with soot and age.

Lavinia often found herself staring at the ceiling in church, not only because the architecture was designed to do just that: first lead the eye upward, with the hope that the soul would follow, but also because she felt voyeuristic observing others in their earnest and sometimes urgent communications with their Lord. In Paris, she'd noticed the whole business of religion was taken more seriously than it had been in New York, where she had not known a single person who went to church on any other day than Sunday, and even then, certain times of the year were spotty and only Christmas and Easter were inviolate.

Looking at the scenes of worldly torment tucked into the dimly lit alcoves was also not an appealing option. The organist was heavy-handed, imparting a lugubrious quality even to the up-tempo pieces, and Lavinia was growing restless. When her neck became sore from craning to look up, she cast her eyes downward, and examined the details of the worn velvet prie-dieu, the nap worn away where knees had rested, leaving behind oblong shadows.

On the floor near her left foot she noticed a prayer card that had fallen between the benches. On one side was a familiar psalm and on the other, a detail from a painting of Saint Jerome. It was not the depiction of Saint Jerome, however, that inspired Lavinia. It was the primitive representation of the lion. The beast had been rendered like a cross between a Chinese temple dragon and a lap dog, looking up at the bearded saint lovingly, paw reaching forward as if begging for a treat, black lips grinning clownishly.

There was a pause as the organist concluded the piece, letting the last reverberations fill the church, the echoes fading into the dark niches that eventually swallowed the sound as fully as they had the light. Lavinia looked up at the highest point of the arch where the last note still fluttered. She recalled, from History of Art at Miss Dillwater's, that Leonardo da Vinci defined the arch as two weaknesses making a strength.

Lavinia looked down at the prayer card, to the little lion at Saint Jerome's feet, unfurling its thin ribbon of tongue like a banner of devotion. Suddenly she understood, with a clarity that could not have been more pronounced had it been accompanied by trumpets and timpani, what she must do.

What she was lacking, she realized, was a companion and a calling. The solution was simple. She would get a pug and have a profession. Lavinia picked up the prayer card and opened her handbag with a crisp snap, releasing the clasp on her bag so that it swung open like a jaw yawning wide to be fed. She inserted the card and clacked the bag closed again with yet another decisive snap.

A ruddy-faced man sitting next to her, exhaling the heavy licorice breath of an anisette drinker, hissed disapprovingly, "Comme c'est mal élevé." Lavinia knew that the term in French carried an insult of considerably greater weight than the English equivalent "badly brought up." It annoyed her out of all proportion, and, withholding the apology she would otherwise have extended, she whispered back, "Blame it on the wolves."

Then Lavinia drew herself up and made her way awkwardly down the pew to the aisle just before the final fugue began. She was almost home when she realized she had tutoyéd the old man, inadvertently insulting him by addressing him as *tu* instead of *vous*, using the form of grammar that conferred intimacy rather than respect.

The idea upset her: she had been rude to someone her father's age. Once, when she was a child, she had heard a man insult her father in the street and she had never forgotten it.

"You bastards think you own the world," the man had said. He was disheveled and his lurching gait had frightened Lavinia as he approached them on the sidewalk near their house. He was young, and looked like he had been crying. His green eyes were rimmed in red and his face was unevenly swollen.

"Lavinia, wait inside the lobby for me," her father commanded, releasing his grip on her hand which was always uncomfortably firm though she never would have dared to complain.

"You wanna know what they call you in the mailroom?" the young man continued, as her father tried to calm him, steering the man away from the entrance to their building, where the uniformed doorman looked on anxiously from behind the glass door, as if calculating the tip he would get if he had to take a swing at an angry drunk. Her father's lips, when he returned to Lavinia a few minutes later, were pressed tightly into a line as thin as a pencil mark and he seemed somehow smaller.

Lavinia had not heard the rest of the exchange but she could see how upset her father was by the episode; he was flushed and when he spoke his voice was ragged.

"Go upstairs and tell Miss Kaye that you will not be going to the zoo after all."

"Why not, Papa? You promised."

Pete, the Irish doorman, had tried to signal to her, shaking his head in warning behind her father's back, his large body useless to protect her in any other way.

"Don't talk back," Mr. Gibbs snapped.

He had taken off his homburg and was fanning himself with it although it was not warm. On her father's forehead a vein was raised and throbbing. He looked ill, drained of color, glistening with a thin veneer of sweat, as though feverish. Lavinia felt queasy too, seeing him so visibly shaken, as if his authority, which she had never questioned, could be diminished by a handful of words flung at him like pebbles by someone half his age, by someone who should have called him "sir." She felt his humiliation spread through her as if it were something contagious.

"Tell your mother I have to go to the office. Something has come up."

"Yes, Papa."

She stared at his shoes, avoiding his eyes; his right spat

was scuffed. She had never seen her father soiled before. In Lavinia's mind the two things fused in a cautionary tale: This was what could happen if you disrespected your elders. It would leave a mark, a visible reproach, a crack in the foundation.

Lavinia suddenly came to a standstill on the narrow sidewalk of the Rue de l'Ancienne Comédie. For a long moment she considered going back. The old man in the church had been right. The words he had hissed through his waxed moustache with the harsh impatience of her father had been true. She was mal élevée, after all.

As she stood on the curb, trying to decide if she should go back and what she might say if she could even find the old man again now that the concert would be letting out, Lavinia sighed and clacked open her handbag again and withdrew the last cigarette from her silver case. She had wanted a smoke throughout the last partitas and now she no longer felt the need to wait until she was home: she would smoke on the street, like workmen and street vendors did.

As she tried to light her cigarette, a gust of wind skittered down the narrow street, carrying with it the smell of sautéed onions from a kitchen vent, and scattering like starlings the leaflets that had collected in the gutter. Some of the sheets of paper had been wadded into tight balls that moved stutteringly over the cobblestones, but the leaflets that were flat skimmed along trying to loft like kites, collecting in doorways and blowing up against Lavinia's ankles.

After several unsuccessful attempts to get the cigarette lit, she stepped into a doorway and turned her back to the street. In the flare of light from her match she noticed, as she took the first of a series of drags deep enough to make her slightly dizzy, the sign on the door. Help wanted. Part-time assistant. Inquire next door at number 37. Ask for Monsieur Druette.

Lavinia had not bothered to save the mimeographed program from the concert so she picked up one of the least smudged leaflets that had collected at her feet and copied down the name and address on the back side of the sheet and then, folding it several times, until it was no larger than a playing card, she slipped it into her now empty cigarette case, where the germs from the street could be quarantined. She had never before picked up litter or taken the political tracts that callused hands proffered at busy intersections. Now she had done both.

It would be difficult, if not impossible, she knew, to get a job through an agency; French companies would always fill a vacancy with a citizen before a foreigner, and a man before a woman. She had no experience or particular gifts that would compel her consideration: her French was merely serviceable, her typing slow and she was already middle-aged. Moreover, she felt guilty about the prospect of taking work from someone who needed it more than she did, just as she had felt guilty when younger, prettier women had eyed her when she had walked arm in arm with Sven, as if she were taking from them something they had more right to and would better appreciate.

Her best chance for employment would be to find an individual willing to let her work off the books. Though she had not yet been in France for a full year, Lavinia already understood how eloquent small sums of cash had been in securing the attention of minor functionaries; most people had a venal side that could be accessed if the proper protocols were observed. Gordon had been right about that. She could afford to work for just enough less to provide an incentive to hire her but she could only take on work in which her employment could be concealed.

Lavinia remembered Mavis complaining frequently about how she was an invisible drudge, arriving after other employees had left, working in back rooms while cleaning crews emptied litter baskets and polished name plates. What Mavis had found isolating and anonymous was exactly what Lavinia required to establish a toehold which she could later parlay into something more rewarding. Even the prospect of the search galvanized her with a sense of purpose.

As Lavinia pushed open the heavy door to her apartment building, she could hear Madame Luberon's voice cutting through the shadows of the arched passage, coming from the kitchen window at which she usually sat like a sentry, observing all who entered with a critical eye. Lavinia hurried past quickly, noticing from the corner of her eye Monsieur

Luberon seated at the small table, eating his dinner. The table was covered with a greasy blue and white checked oilcloth and flypaper dangled from the single bulb that illuminated his meal. Monsieur Luberon was shaking his head dismissively, sawing at a lump of gray meat with a large pocket knife, cutlery being an unnecessary nicety.

As if addressing Lavinia's thoughts, Madame Luberon was angrily, loudly insisting that her husband join a protest at the Place de la Concorde against the foreign parasites, Communists and Jews ruining the country, taking away the few jobs that still remained. A placard with the slogan "France aux Français" leaned against their door, waiting to be raised skyward.

The pug proved easier to find than employment. Lavinia had begun to play backgammon with the wife of one of the American deputy consuls, having relaxed her prohibition on expats around the holidays when she'd allowed herself to attend a few parties at the Embassy. She was grateful for her immediate welcome and happy to be a fourth for bridge or a companion for matinees, or to sing in the chorus of Gilbert and Sullivan theatricals organized by the vice deputy's wife. Lavinia discovered among them a collection of women with whom she could swap books and have lunch from time to time in the Bois de Boulogne. A few she liked well enough, such as Anne Aubretton and Lorraine Tyson, for ski weekends in Austria or sightseeing excursions to Mont Saint-Michel or Azay-le-Rideau. In Alice Baker, however, Lavinia found a close friend.

Alice Baker was very delicate with huge blue eyes that gave her a cartoonish air of innocence she exploited whenever possible. She had a husband, older by two decades, a parrot and four dogs, one of which was a pug. It was Alice Baker's love of animals, in fact, that had secured Lavinia's friendship. Two of Alice's dogs were blind, and the greyhound had been rescued from the track at Deauville.

There was a litter, Alice said, waving away the maid who had just served them hot chocolate, that her butcher was trying to place.

"Of course, he can't keep them, *le pauvre*, but he has a heart. Always gives me extra bones for my little ones," Alice went on, rubbing the head of an obese black poodle nestling at her feet.

"He's promised his daughter to wait until they are weaned, so she has a chance to find them homes. But it won't be easy. They have no pedigree I'm afraid. I hope that doesn't deter you."

"My own has never done me much good," Lavinia replied, making Alice laugh and spill her hot chocolate on the lace tablecloth.

"Don't let the servants hear you say that," Alice cautioned with a wink as she rang the bell for Lisette, "We've enough trouble with them as it is."

She folded her napkin over the spreading stain and raised her hands in mock helplessness. Though she was much younger than her husband, it was said that she couldn't have

children. Watching Alice feed a glazed petit four to the greyhound, and then lift her finger to her lips conspiratorially,
since her husband vociferously forbade this, Lavinia wondered if Alice's solution to not having children was to stay one
herself.

"It's not a concern of mine," Lavinia repeated. It was frus-
trating to her that she always sounded so serious around
Alice, unable to summon even an intimation of humor in her
presence, as if Alice somehow laid claim to all the levity her
drawing room could contain.

"Well, I'm glad to hear it," Alice said, wrinkling her freckled nose. "Bloodlines were all anyone was talking about in
Berlin when we were at the Olympic games. It just about
ruined our vacation. Harold thinks we should all be mixed up
at birth. That way, we'd all be bound together by love, not separated by blood. Silly, isn't it? But also oddly brilliant, just like
Harold." She laughed and pushed her chair back and rose.

"Come," she said, holding out her hand for Lavinia, "let's
go find you a puppy. Frankly, what with things being as they
are, I'm afraid someone will take them home and make a tasty
stew, just like they did during the Paris Commune." She bent
down to nuzzle her own pug dog. "Right, Moumou?" she
cooed, letting the little black face lick her hand frantically,
searching for a sweet. "Someone might make a little Moumou
ragout!"

Lavinia was usually embarrassed when adults spoke in
baby talk but Alice escaped censure. Like the conversation

one might overhear a child having with a doll, there was
something winning about her lack of self-consciousness as
she discoursed in silly voices with her different pets, oblivious
to the judgment of others. Lavinia was also amused by the
way the little dog turned its head to the side, the bulging gar-
goyle eyes beseeching, a paw raised in supplication as if
responding to what had been said.

Lavinia couldn't help herself. She knelt down, running a
stocking in the process, and reassured Moumou, "Don't listen
to a word she says. Such a thing could never happen," Lavinia
counseled. She felt foolish almost immediately, not because
of how she had inflected her voice, but because she had spoken to the animal as though it were a child, and that seemed
even more ludicrous. She stood up quickly and bumped
against a chair, nearly knocking it over.

"Oopsadaisy," Alice said kindly, but that only made
Lavinia more aware of how awkward she felt just then, tow-
ering over her diminutive hostess, her stocking laddering
down past the hem of her dress. It wasn't until they were in
the back of Alice's Daimler, winding their way through the
less affluent arrondissements of the Right Bank, that Lavinia
recovered her composure.

"Of course, I'm just dying to see Josephine Baker," Alice
was saying. She had been chattering continuously since they
got into the car. "I must be the only person in Paris who
hasn't, but I just can't persuade Harold to take me. He's been
teased too much. Every would-be wit asking if he's related,

elbow in the side, 'kissing cousins,' wink, wink, 'black sheep of the family.' You can just imagine the drift. He's plain lost his sense of humor about it."

Lavinia didn't think Harold had much of a sense of humor to begin with, but she just nodded, and smiled and wished her own humor was more in evidence, though it was only a passing thought, not a piercing one. One of the appealing features of Alice's company, besides her capacity to laugh and her oddball enthusiasms, was her genuine kindness; Alice never seemed to notice Lavinia's failings. There had been a time in Lavinia's life when she might have mistaken this for complacency or weakness but now she was merely grateful. She stretched out her long legs and sighed and let content-ment surge through her like a shot of Armagnac, savoring the feeling of expansiveness that rose up giddily in her chest, like a trapped laugh.

Out of the window she watched the rows of ancient build-ings sagging crookedly against each other, the venerable beauty of their decrepitude marred only by the occasional drape of wash hung from a window rail or balcony. As the chauffeur steered them down the twisting streets to the home of Monsieur Minon, the butcher, and the puppy waiting for her to claim it, Lavinia mentioned her interest in finding work.

"There's plenty of volunteer work to be had, believe me," Alice responded brightly, "all those refugees seeping in from Spain and Germany. Harold says they're mostly Gypsies but still, they need all *kinds* of help. Just think about the little ones. . . ." Alice trailed off, clearly not wanting to do the very thing she recommended. "Besides, I thought you were already giving the Ladies Brigade two afternoons a week."

"I was actually not thinking about volunteer work," Lavinia said quickly, not wanting Alice to lose her buoyancy, which sometimes seemed alarmingly fragile.

"You mean have a business? Like that Beach woman with the moldy bookstore and lesbian friends?" Alice laughed, recovering her ingénue's delight. Then she arched her pale eyebrows with genuine concern.

"You still have your income, haven't you?" she whispered discreetly, even though the glass partition separating them from the chauffeur was always raised because Harold's job required privacy.

"Oh no, it's nothing like that," Lavinia hastened to reassure her, knowing full well that if she *had* been in need of money she would never have asked nor would Alice ever have given it. They were very close, but not close enough for money to pass between them. She was relieved, however, that the conversation was interrupted by their arrival at the undistinguished building in which the butcher made his home.

The chauffeur pulled the Daimler up onto the sidewalk and then stepped out of the car to press the door buzzer while the ladies waited in the backseat. After a few minutes, Sévérine Minon, a skinny eight-year-old in a Catholic school uniform, brought down the squirming, yapping puppies in a wicker basket and placed them in the capacious footwell of the backseat.

Lavinia knew at once which one she wanted; it was Alice who detained them for almost half an hour while she nuzzled each of them, cradling them in succession in her arms like an infant, and letting them climb on the leather seat and snag the expensive fabric of her dress.

"Do you think Harold would ever forgive me if I brought one home?" Alice asked, but Lavinia was spared having to render a judgment. One of the puppies started to pee in the car and that brought Alice back to her senses as quickly as a slap. She tried to hold the tiny thing out of the window so as to direct the stream of urine into the street, but it was squirming, paddling in the air with its paws, splattering the car door and the little girl standing beside it, who had been regarding herself in its reflecting sheen.

The chauffeur, who had been waiting across the street, leaning against the wall smoking a Gitane, rushed over immediately. Without the slightest flicker of expression, he removed first the incontinent puppy from Alice's hands, and then the wicker basket with the rest of them, which he relayed into the arms of the little girl whose face by contrast with his own was a maelstrom of emotion.

"Oh dear," Alice fretted, daubing at her blouse with a handkerchief. "I hope it's not ruined. I've only worn it once." The chauffeur had already extracted some rags from the trunk and was wiping down the car door with short, quick movements that conveyed an annoyance he could never voice. He had handed Lavinia a newspaper for her lap before he gave her the puppy back, its paws rubbed clean with his handkerchief, which he did not return to his pocket but to the trunk of the car. When he had finished cleaning the Daimler's door and returned to the driver's seat, Alice leaned across the backseat and cupped her hand around Lavinia's ear, whispering breathily, "He's not supposed to smoke on the job. He burned a hole in one of the uniforms and Harold had a fit because they're tailored in London. Also, it's unseemly, but I think the expense is what really bothered Harold. I never say anything though."

Then Alice slid over to her side of the backseat and looked at her watch and sighed. "We'd better get back. It's almost time for cocktails. The Dunbarts are stopping by for dinner and so is Theodora Althorp, and I can't stand her. I'd make you stay but you need to get your little friend home."

Alice rapped on the glass for the chauffeur's attention and when he turned around she held up her coin purse and pointed at the little girl who stood on the sidewalk, still holding the wicker basket of puppies. Alice lowered the partition and instructed the chauffeur to give her something.

Dutifully, he got back out of the car and walked around to the curb and unceremoniously dropped a few francs into the basket, as if giving alms to a beggar. Séverine Minon's lip was puffed out and trembling, and she was doing her best not to cry. Suddenly Lavinia knew she had taken the little girl's favorite.

"I should have known you'd pick the runt, Lavinia," Alice said, rolling down her window. Then she leaned her head out slightly and said to the chauffeur, "Encore plus," and the chauffeur reluctantly withdrew from his pocket more coins, dropping them into the basket one by one, looking back at Alice every few francs until the sum was sufficient and Alice nodded her head.

As the car drove off, Alice reached out her hands for the pug settled in Lavinia's lap. "Okay, let's see what you've got there," she said, and Lavinia handed her the little dog because she couldn't very well say no, no matter how much she wanted to. Her lap was warm where its belly had pressed against her, emanating the smell of wet hay, and old shoe, which Lavinia associated with truffles and the dark crumbly earth in which they were found. As she lifted up the puppy to give it to Alice, it felt so small and defenseless, snuffling at her hand in confusion and breathing moistly on her fingers, that Lavinia felt a pang of anger at Alice for disturbing it.

Alice examined the dog's rear and said matter-of-factly, "It's a boy. Do you have any idea of what you'll name him?" She picked a shred of newspaper off the pad of a back paw and added, "and the little fellow is a Communist, judging from what he reads. Harold says you can tell the politics of a café by what newspapers are torn in strips for use in the WC. It's the management's way of disrespecting the views it doesn't like. Do you think that could be true? It doesn't sound at all clean!"

Alice kissed the dog's snout and handed it back to Lavinia, who was perched awkwardly, trying to look casual, her hands itching to have the animal back.

"Look," Alice said, "the little thing can't take its eyes off of you. I'll bet it won't let you out of sight once you get it home." Lavinia smiled. "Then I guess I'll have to call him Boswell," she said.

With Boswell, Lavinia discovered a kind of love she had not expected to feel once the possibility of children became improbable. Because he was the runt of the litter, Boswell was sickly, and required in his first few months all the care of an infant. Lavinia gave him medicine from an eyedropper and boiled chickens down to a dark broth to fortify his food. She spent afternoons with him on her lap, wrapped in a cashmere sweater, while she waited in the outer room of the veterinarian's office.

She paid close attention to his stools, monitoring their consistency and color for clues to his health, noting the amount of water he passed and checking his weight every day by weighing herself twice, first without Boswell and then with him. She boiled rice and pressed it through a strainer and fed it to him on her finger tip when he wouldn't eat his food. Boswell repaid her devotion by becoming her shadow.

Even Madame Luberon was moved to comment on it: "C'est pas normal, ça! Il est comme un petit amant" she said, noting his ardent attention to Lavinia, and there was an air of wistfulness lurking behind her usual bristle. Eventually, and it took many months, Madame Luberon began patting Boswell on the head while Lavinia collected her mail. Madame Luberon bent over heavily and when she was as close as she could get to eye level, she told Boswell how monstrous his looks were while she scratched his ear, making his corkscrew tail vibrate with pleasure. From then on, Madame Luberon never failed to greet "Le petit monstre" as she called him, lavishing an affection on the dog that never managed to increase her civility to Lavinia.

By then, Lavinia didn't care. She had learned not to take any of the rudenesses to heart. She had come to recognize it as a kind of game the French liked to play. It was a form of hostile flirtation, creating an intimacy while maintaining a pointed privacy. As with bargaining, the better the opponent the more entertaining the sport was. The less she cared, the more respect Madame Luberon felt for her which could only be expressed through further rudeness.

Monsieur Druette, at number 37, had been rude too, when Lavinia had inquired about the note he'd written advertising a position for an assistant. Monsieur Druette, however, was brusque in a dismissive way that did not suggest a desire to engage wills. Not only did he refuse to give Lavinia work, he refused to even tell her what kind of work she was being denied. "C'est impossible," he said, explaining no further. Lavinia persisted. She no longer was considering the possibility of the work—Monsieur Druette was clearly such an unpleasant type no wage would be adequate inducement to return, but it infuriated her to be treated ill by him.

Monsieur Druette, sallow and bitter, bent in the slouch that marked so many functionaries in the lower bowels of government, was an easy type for Lavinia to bully because she could sense a fear of assertive women. She stood in front of the door and stared him down while he gesticulated his regrets, wagging his head and shrugging his shoulders, palms up. Lavinia knew that if she were to be imperious he would wilt. She was better dressed than he; his suit was shiny with wear, his shirt frayed at the collar, but more intimidating perhaps, she was significantly taller. Finally, to be rid of her, Monsieur Druette gave Lavinia the name of a man he had run across who had in the past needed an assistant and, for all Druette knew, might still.

In truth, the connection was a glancing one. Monsieur Druette had sold a set of antique tin soldiers to a man who had offered twice the amount Monsieur Druette had hoped to get at the flea market. The scrap of paper with his name and address had been saved in a desk drawer in case Monsieur Druette came across more bric-a-brac he could sell to the man at an unreasonable price, but it had never happened. He'd forgotten it until now.

Nonetheless Martin Druette was pleased to have safeguarded the address. He was a man who prided himself on his frugality. He saved the tin lids from cans and the paper sleeves in which baguettes were sold. Monsieur Druette had a box in which he saved bits of string and rubber bands, which he cut in two if they were thick enough to allow duplication. His wife had labeled the box "Bits of string too small to use," but Monsieur Druette believed that sooner or later, everything had its use.

"To assist at what kind of work?" Lavinia asked, as Monsieur Druette hurriedly copied out the address. He sighed with irritation. He couldn't remember what kind of assistant it was the man had mentioned he was looking for. The remark had been made in passing and hadn't been of concern until now, when it had suddenly become useful. He handed her the man's coordinates, written in small tight letters using as little ink as possible, on a scrap of brown paper which, judging from the odor, had recently wrapped a pungent cheese. Lavinia instinctively lifted the torn corner of paper to her nose to have a deeper whiff, but Monsieur Druette interpreted this action as a reproach.

"Oh-la-la," he countered gutturally, rolling his eyes, and puffing air through his lips, "do you want me to write it on my shirt perhaps? Would that please you, Madame?" he demanded, as he ushered her out of his establishment, opening the door so violently the glass panes rattled. Lavinia would have tried to explain, to say something to mollify him and certainly she would have thanked him had she not been choking back the laughter she knew might erupt if she as much as opened her mouth.

She had never actually heard a Frenchman say "oh la la" before, though its use in caricature just like the beret or baguette, was everywhere in evidence. But the three non-sense syllables, like a magic charm, released an explosive, childish hilarity, as if uncorking the exaggerated passions enacted by the Grand Guignol puppets on Saturday mornings in the Tuilleries. Her mistake had been to let herself imagine Monsieur Druette in the costume of Gendarme, wielding his oversized baton.

When Lavinia got back to her apartment she took the scrap of brown paper out of her handbag, which had begun to smell like cheese, and put it in the icebox, next to a jar of cornichons. It languished there for months, soggy and forgotten. Lavinia distracted herself with Anne Aubretton and Alice Baker and her new circle of friends, allowing them to enlist her for the various causes they championed, all of which were worthy if not compelling. It gave her an immediate sense of community and she noticed with amusement that among the expats, the worse their French, the more fervently they welcomed her to the fold.

When the telegram arrived announcing her mother's imminent arrival, Lavinia found herself charged with childish glee and nervous energy, the combination of emotions that had dominated the days before Christmas when she was little, infusing her with a buzzing feeling that was both pleasant and unpleasant, like being tickled too long. Mrs. Gibbs was traveling with Gordon and his wife on the *S.S. Normandy* and would be staying in the Place Vendôme.

"Father can't come. Next time for sure" was the only reference made to the conspicuous absence of her father. Lavinia had read the telegram over and over, smoking cigarette after cigarette, as if there were still more for the yellow foolscap to reveal. It was not clear to her if her father's absence indicated censure or circumstance. She could readily imagine that he was still nursing his indignation; her broken engagement had cast in a questionable light business dealings between Shelby and Mr. Gibbs.

In the months following the announcement of the engagement, Mr. Gibbs had taken a significant sum of money from Shelby to invest in the stocks that Mr. Gibbs's firm represented. When the engagement was broken, the money was not immediately available and the investment began to look suspect. It was repaid, of course, and Shelby had done well when the deal was ultimately concluded. In the intervening months, however, Mr. Gibbs had had to suffer the whispers and rumors that stained the reputation he had so carefully built on the floor of the Exchange.

"If any man had besmirched my reputation to the extent my daughter has, he would have lost his teeth," was what he had told his sons, and they repeated it to Lavinia.

"Because you are headstrong and selfish you have made what our family did out of generosity look like greed. Father would never have allowed an outside investor to take part in that deal. It was only because your impending marriage gave Shelby the privileges of family. And guess what, Lavinia," Gordon had added theatrically, "even though he'll make a bundle, that's not what gets remembered."

It was also possible that her father was choosing to take advantage of the opportunity to enjoy the rare pleasure of solitude. Early in his marriage, he had been reluctant to leave his beautiful wife alone for fear he would lose her to a poacher. Later, she was reluctant to leave him alone because she had discovered he had a mistress. Even after the affair had ended, Mrs. Gibbs maintained a scrupulous accounting for her husband's whereabouts, managing his time like a miser hoarding the final coins of a lost fortune.

"I think at this point, Father's idea of a holiday is a vacation from Mother," Grace had once remarked, based only on the fact that at a luncheon party Mr. Gibbs had interrupted his wife in the middle of an anecdote by saying briskly, as he signaled for the soup plates to be cleared, "I'm sure everyone here has heard this story before, Eliza, and we don't want to tax their goodwill."

Grace would have been devastated to learn of her father's infidelity; she had enough trouble sharing his attention with her mother and siblings, and while she might adopt a posture of offended rectitude, the truth was that it would have made her jealous. Lavinia therefore never told Grace about the argument she had heard rise up the chimney flue one night at the summer house, when all the children were supposed to be asleep, the sharp sibilant hisses conveying an anger all the more powerful for having been constrained in whispers.

There were many secrets Lavinia had kept over the years. She'd never told anyone about what she saw Ambrose doing to a chambermaid at the Gritti Palace in Venice the summer they had toured Europe as a family or that it was Gordon who had stolen the envelope with cash for Christmas bonuses her father had brought home to distribute among their own servants and those who worked for the building. It was not a huge sum of money. Mr. Gibbs did not believe in lavish tips: it encouraged indolence and expectation. The housekeeper had been fired and the incident was quickly forgotten. But not by Lavinia. She had known too which servants had taken bottles of wine from the pantry or change from the silver bowl on Ambrose's dresser, or used her mother's perfume before heading out on their one day off a week, but she said nothing. Lavinia wondered from time to time what secret things her siblings knew that she didn't; she imagined them all working on separate jigsaw puzzles that would never be complete.

The prospect of the family visit filled Lavinia with excitement and dread in alternating rushes. Suddenly, there was no time for anything but the preparation for their arrival. Lavinia retreated to the claw-foot bathtub making lists until her fingertips were as dimpled as overcooked peas. She wrote down topics to be avoided, and questions to ask, sights to see, and lists of last-minute improvements to be made to her apartment or herself.

She bought the missing niceties her mother would expect to see if she came to inspect the apartment, such as a bedspread and curtains, and hand towels, although Lavinia knew there was no way to gild the truth; Mrs. Gibbs would be horrified by her bohemian lifestyle even though by Parisian standards it qualified as privileged. A housekeeper and a laundress were features that set her well above the average Parisian in

the 1930s but these were details not likely to impress her
mother as anything but the most basic necessities.

When the second telegram arrived, this time from the
Savoy in London, Lavinia was not entirely surprised to learn
that the itinerary had changed and the Paris leg of the trip
had been severed. Twice before there had been discussions of
a visit that never materialized. Each time she'd get stirred up,
her heart answering an ancient call, but by the end of her second year abroad, the pull her family had over her had diminished significantly. She thought of herself as a falconer's hawk,
after the hood has been discarded and it's been set loose.
Often they died in the wild but she hadn't. She'd learned to
hunt for herself and now if she returned to the leather glove
it was by choice.

> *At the Savoy.*
> *Holding a room for you.*
> *Join us here.*
> *Explanation to follow.*

The telegram was signed by Gordon and he never bothered to provide much of an explanation, even when questioned in person. He met her at Dover with a car and driver
and muttered something about his wife's sensitive stomach
and how taxing it had been for her traveling beyond the
realm of the English language. Almost immediately after he

had secured Lavinia's luggage and settled her into the back-seat of the car, he nodded off, dozing lightly throughout the rainy drive to London. As the afternoon advanced, the sky became increasingly mottled, darkening unevenly like a bruise, and Lavinia felt an old familiar sadness seeping into her heart.

She watched Gordon sleep, his jaw slack and open, his head hanging to the side at an angle that looked uncomfortable. She resisted the urge to reach over and tilt his head back against the leather upholstery because she thought about how awkward it would be if he awoke. Gordon had never liked certain kinds of physical contact and on the occasions when she had hugged him she could feel him stiffen as if to withstand something painful, though as a boy he and Ambrose and Jasper used to endure tests of manhood that often involved candle flames and penknives.

Lavinia noticed how he had thickened in the time she'd been away and how the corners of his mouth now turned down, even when he was relaxed, giving his face a sterner cast which she imagined he must use to advantage against his legal adversaries. He was still a handsome man but he had become forbidding; now his even features seemed only to further the sense of inaccessibility. Like the cold beauty of a statue, his features commanded admiration but in no way invited approach.

She was glad she had not brought Boswell, much as it had

pained her to leave him with Alice for the extended weekend. It was their first separation and he had whimpered piteously at her departure. The sound of his cries haunted her halfway across the Channel, but she could see now how easily Boswell would have become a convenient scapegoat for unspoken resentments. Gordon's anger, which had always been present as a child, had not been tempered by maturity or success. On the contrary, though he had been among the few who had managed to multiply their fortunes during the years that followed the '29 crash, he seemed to have acquired with his wealth a bitterness that wearied him and sapped the joy he had previously taken from his professional life.

When they finally arrived at the hotel, Mrs. Gibbs was out with Gordon's wife, Constance. Gordon went straight up to his room, leaving Lavinia with several hours to fill before dinner. She chose to wander the streets looking in store windows rather than wait alone in her room for the appointed hour at which the Gibbses would gather for a meal in the hotel's dining room. She was exhausted from her trip; the Channel crossing had not been difficult, but making conversation with Gordon once he awoke had been exceedingly so. Lavinia knew enough about dread to know that sitting still exacerbated it, allowing it to pool in the stomach and pound in the chest; the only cure was movement. Now that she'd arrived, the whole idea of the visit seemed obviously wrong and easily avoided.

• • •

During her four days in London, Lavinia saw very little of her sister-in-law, though when she *was* in evidence, Constance was just as Lavinia remembered: meticulous in dress and distant in her conversation. Gordon's wife was pretty and poised, but tight, like an overstretched rubber band on the verge of snapping. Lavinia understood Constance had been having health problems, though it was never completely clear if her illness was the result of the miscarriage or the cause of it. In any case, her absence from the outing to the National Gallery and several meals was not felt by Lavinia to be a significant loss.

It was her mother's change that most affected Lavinia. Mrs. Gibbs seemed to have become old, unaccountably old, in the time Lavinia had been away. Her hands betrayed her the most markedly, now foxed with brown and having acquired a slight tremble. Her body, too, seemed withered and she no longer held herself with the imperious pride that had underscored her looks well past the loss of her youth.

It was not just the physical decline that alarmed Lavinia, the way Mrs. Gibbs slumped in her chair between courses as if too fatigued for good posture or that she was either oblivious or indifferent to the fleck of sauce that decorated her chin until finally Gordon flapped his napkin at her with an impatient remark. It was the way in which her mother had become vague and sweet that caused Lavinia to cry in her hotel room each night. Lavinia no longer recognized in her mother the woman whose love had seemed as impossible to hold, and yet as necessary to have, as air.

The visit could be deemed a success only because Lavinia was determined to make it so and because it was of very short duration. There were several moments that had threatened to erupt into ugliness, but Lavinia had managed to quell them. She had been prepared for an inevitable confrontation with Gordon or his snippy wife, and even had looked forward to it the way a soldier waiting for attack yearns for the release that comes in the discharge of his weapon. However, the confused, panicky look on her mother's face when tempers flared around her dissuaded Lavinia from pursuing provocations that littered her family's discourse like shards of glass hidden in a luxurious lawn.

On one occasion when an exchange between Gordon and Lavinia had become fraught, Mrs. Gibbs clutched Gordon's arm as if for support, but rather than linking herself to him at the elbow, she pushed her head up under his arm as though trying to disappear beneath his wing. "Mother!" he had exclaimed, but the argument had instantly been dropped.

Another time, still more upsetting to Lavinia, Gordon had insulted the present she had brought from Paris for his son, Spencer. It had taken Lavinia a considerable effort to find the harlequin puppet with a hand-painted wooden head. Gordon refused to take it home. "I don't want you to pollute my son with your moral indolence. He doesn't need dolls and I won't let you make him into a fairy." His voice was sharp and wounding and Lavinia's mother had lifted her napkin up to cover her face, hiding with the ineptitude of a child much younger than the one under discussion. As Lavinia rose and excused herself from the table, Gordon said, "Don't be such a spoilsport, Mongo. I'll give him something else and say that it was from you," but it was not his rudeness that had moved her to tears.

When Lavinia said good-bye to her family the following day in the hotel lobby, once again she felt herself struggling to reconcile competing and conflicting emotions. She was almost dumbstruck with a sense of impending loss and giddy at the prospect of escape. Though Gordon had tried to persuade her to return home, invoking the political unrest on the continent, Lavinia knew she would not be leaving Paris anytime in the foreseeable future.

By the time the Germans occupied Poland, Alice and her menagerie were long gone from Paris. As soon as Germany annexed Austria, Harold had suggested Alice return to the States, but in November of 1938, when the teletype report of Kristallnacht passed through his hands, he insisted Alice return to the States by the end of the year. "It will only get worse in thirty-nine. Look at the momentum that Hitler's built just in these last six months."

In the past, Harold had often seemed embarrassed by his posting, by the fact that some of the ministries and government departments he had occasion to contact still used calligraphers for accreditation and had no dictation machines in their offices. "Paris is pretty, but it's not London. Paris is a place you go to honeymoon, not to change the world," he'd complained. But that had been several years ago, when the only thing Americans had to fear in France was the falling exchange rate and indigestion.

Now that Paris was no longer a honeymoon destination and Europe was convulsing with turmoil, Harold no longer wanted to change the world. Vom Rath, secretary of the German Embassy in Paris, had been shot, and in response to the pogroms in Germany, U.S. relations with Germany had been strained. All that year there'd been grousing within the foreign service at the tedious extra work caused by the refugees, not to mention the stolen and forged passports which were being sold on the black market to German and Austrian Jews. Harold had always expected to retire at the end of the decade, but now the prospect of cutting his career short by a matter of months did not seem soon enough. By the time his transfer came through, most Americans had fled the continent. Harold urged Lavinia to leave as well.

He had taken her to a brasserie famous for its choucroute and the smell of vinegar filled the crowded room. In the smoked mirror that lined the walls she could see the back of his head, his gray hair surrounding a small pink bald spot, and it made her feel a rush of tenderness.

"It's not wise to be abroad now. And for a woman alone I think it's madness. Once I'm gone you'll have no one to help you when you need it. Don't be headstrong, my dear. I can get you passage on a boat now if you let me."

Lavinia declined his offer and though it was repeated

twice more, each time with increasing urgency, she insisted she *was* home and she did feel safe, and she had just had her floors sanded.

She was enormously moved by Harold's concern; he was so clearly agitated. All the signs, the way he tugged on his earlobe and chewed on the inside of his cheek, the way he fingered his Phi Beta Kappa key, they were all familiar to her. She had joined Alice from time to time in finding amusement in his habits and tics.

"Just watch. I'll bet I can get him to stutter if I really try," Alice had from time to time boasted, at functions that bored her, or if she felt Harold had ignored her in favor of some inconsequential second-tier diplomat or if he had denied Alice a small pleasure or a bauble for which she hankered. Now, watching him suffer on her behalf, stirred by his sense of duty and affection, Lavinia was sorry she had ever enjoyed a laugh at his expense, or avoided him at the cocktail hour in favor of someone whose conversation had more verve.

Harold waited for her reply. She wanted not to disappoint him. He had been disappointed enough; she could see it in his weary eyes, his puffy hands with his perfectly manicured fingernails. He lit their cigarettes, signaled for the check, and cleared his throat, which was another of his habits about which Alice liked to tease him.

"Well then," he said.

"Harold," Lavinia started, but the words she had formulated evaporated in her mouth and in their place there was only a dryness she could not swallow away. He had risen and was holding her coat for her. His whole body seemed weighted with resignation, as if he had already added her to the list of people he could not save, gestures that were, in the end, sterile.

On the street, in front of his car, Harold put out his hand in parting and she clasped it in both of hers in a display of affection that startled both of them. Lavinia brought his gloved hand to her lips, and gave it a quick kiss, just lightly grazing the calf's skin, which seemed as soft and warm as the lips for which it was a proxy.

"I can't leave," she said, still holding his hand in hers. "I'm in love."

"Poor dear," was his reply. Lavinia let go of his hand and he used it to pat her awkwardly on the shoulder, for suddenly tears were streaking her face, glinting in the headlights of passing traffic.

"I don't suppose I should ask," he said.

"Ever the diplomat," Lavinia admired, wiping her nose with the handkerchief he proffered. There was something so comforting about the smell of his cologne on the starched cotton that she almost felt sleepy and confessional.

"Does Alice know?"

"No one knows."

"Then I'll guard your secret with my life," Harold said theatrically.

"No," Lavinia replied, giving her nose a blow, "that's much too high a price for my honor. But I do appreciate your discretion."

"All in a day's work." Harold beamed. He had once complained to her that his was the only profession, besides perhaps undertaking and the clergy, that required such a high degree of reserve and because such was the nature of gratitude, the cost of that reserve was rarely acknowledged. Lavinia smiled at him. His satisfaction was so pure it was charming and contagious. He was puffed up like a pigeon; his overcoat strained to accommodate his rare indulgence in professional pride.

Lavinia refused Harold's offer to be dropped off in the Daimler. She was only a few blocks from home and she wanted to part quickly, cleanly, in front of the restaurant rather than at her door, because the few minutes in the car would have felt interminable, would have muddied the lovely moment she had shared with Harold, which she wanted to save as their last note. In the winter sky, clouds hung low over the roof tops in painterly clusters, their undersides purples and inky blue, and the air smelled of snow. Black slivers of church spires pierced the clotting sky, as if cracking it open to reveal the pentimento of an even darker night. Paris had never been so breathtaking.

As the Daimler drove Harold away, receding down the narrow cobblestones of the Rue Varenne, Lavinia waved once, a formal, perfunctory gesture, but she kept her hand raised and did not bring it down to her side until the car was gone and her fingers were numb. Her coat felt flimsy against the wind coming off the Seine and her shoes hurt and she felt for the first time since she'd left home a frisson of real fear.

She would often, in the following years, think of that image: the pink dot of baldness on the back of Harold's head, framed by the rear window, receding like a pale oval in darkness, an open mouth calling out a message she couldn't hear and wouldn't heed anyway.

TWO

Gaston Lesseur was an unlikely lothario, permanently rumpled, and prematurely jowled, with a slight limp in his left leg which he exaggerated when expedient. The injury was from an accident in his boyhood at a British public school, in a rugby skirmish, but the provenance of the limp was rarely discussed. If the wrong assumptions were made and the injury was ascribed a more heroic origin, Gaston Lesseur made no effort to correct it.

Those two years in England with his mother were rarely spoken of, and then only in a thin and telegraphic way, as if time could be compressed into the compact elegance of a haiku, discouraging further questions. Since he had returned to France as a teenager and graduated from French schools, the only evidence he'd ever lived among the British was the flawless accent with which he spoke his occasionally flawed English.

Gaston Lesseur kept his brown curls always a little too long and unruly, as if deliberately invoking Byron, and he flaunted a sensuality which experience had taught him was an even greater asset with women than the handsome face and additional height he had yearned for as an adolescent, when even the name Gaston was an embarrassment to him, a reminder of his grandfather's peasant origins. As his confidence grew, so had his vanity, but he had managed to disguise this failing by misdirection, like a prestidigitator at a country fair, directing attention elsewhere while his tongue worked its wiles.

Gaston Lesseur had the kind of charisma that made him popular with men, too, and this he found even more flattering to his ego than his successes with women. Although he wasn't sporty himself, he was a favorite among men who were. His clubhouse sparkle secured his welcome as surely as a distinguished performance on the field or green might have, and his humor was just irreverent enough to be admired without actually being daring enough to offend.

In his early twenties he had married a volatile Italian girl with whom he fought constantly and to whom he was repeatedly unfaithful. She had sullen lips that were the particular pink he associated with erect nipples, making her already voluptuous beauty seem almost obscene and obsessing him in a way he found vaguely humiliating.

Her family owned vineyards in Umbria and treated Gaston with contempt, suspecting he was more interested in their money than in their daughter. They felt his mixed parentage, French father and English mother, had produced in him the worst of both nationalities, and it suggested that he was not well born.

"It never speaks well of a man to raise himself on his wife's back. You would be wasted on him. One doesn't use a thoroughbred to pull a cart," her father said, leaving it to her mother to amplify and embroider the theme at length. If they hadn't tried so strenuously to prevent the union, Carolina Ruffio would never have eloped with a man she had not known long enough to watch a single season's change.

Nevertheless, when Carolina hemorrhaged to death delivering a stillborn son two years into the marriage, Gaston's grief was so obviously authentic her family was both moved and embarrassed. Even the oldest of Carolina's brothers, the one who had, upon meeting, embraced Gaston, hugging him in close only to bite his ear, quick and sharp, like a bird, drawing blood but not attention, even Alessandro Ruffio had come to pity Gaston for the way the loss unmanned him.

Only the cook's fifteen-year-old nephew with the funny eye, who ran errands and raked the gravel walks, remained untouched by the extravagance of his mourning.

"This way, you'll never see her get fat or grow a moustache and you still have something to cry over," he had said to Gaston in exchange for a swig from his flask. "Think how many tears you'd shed when you came to hate her all the time, instead of just some of the time." The comment was wounding and memorable not because it was cruel or blunt, but because Gaston knew it was true.

When Gaston Lesseur finally returned to Paris, it was a day before his twenty-sixth birthday. Instead of a bride, he brought back from Italy a case of particularly fine vintage wine, Carolina's silver rosary beads that had been kissed by the Pope, and just enough of the Ruffio family money to pretend that he was wealthy. None of it, however, gave him much pleasure, not even the unexpected allure the word *widower* conferred, making available to him women who would otherwise have dismissed him as the scoundrel that he was.

Gaston returned to the bank just off the Place Vendôme where he had worked before the detour of his marriage and he was given a position with more prestige and less work than the one he'd left. For a while he had contented himself with women he didn't bother courting and indulgent lunches and purchases that bordered on foppish. He went out for the occasional raucous dinner with male friends who had remained single and could be persuaded to stay out late or play cards for stakes or just get drunk enough to regret it the next day. There were a few obligatory romantic dalliances with suitable women, but Gaston found the pleasure he took from them was never worth the effort required to extricate himself later.

When morale flagged, and the thinness of his social fabric became depressingly evident, Gaston joined a few exclusive clubs to reassure himself that he could, and to take refuge in a sense of community that made no demands but the annual membership fee. He cultivated his appreciation of small but dependable distractions like cigars and backgammon, and subscribed to journals devoted to the minutiae of his various and sometimes obscure interests. By the time Gaston proposed to Céleste Feydeau, he had put on a few kilos and begun to collect the toy soldiers he had loved as a boy and which had been discarded by his mother when he went off to boarding school.

His second marriage, to a petite Frenchwoman who was pale and shy and stuttered when she was nervous, was so obviously the antithesis of his first that Gaston found himself making preemptive remarks about it to his friends. But the tone was never quite right and always sounded more defensive than protective, which he recognized unhappily furthered the assumptions he wished to dispel.

Céleste came from the lesser branch of an almost grand family who liked to trace themselves to the periphery of the Valois line of the throne, but because of her upbringing in the Dordogne, there always clung to her a whiff of the provinces, no matter how fine her clothes and hair. What she lacked in sophistication, however, she replaced with an earnest desire to please. She adored Gaston with dog-like devotion, always following him with her eyes, like a concerned spaniel. She laughed at all his jokes equally, and thought even his most banal remarks were brilliant. She mirrored his opinions unquestioningly, content to follow wherever he led her. He had never been loved like that before and initially Gaston found it irresistible. He had been married to Céleste for seventeen years when he met Lavinia in 1937.

He was on the floor, on his knees, when Lavinia first saw him, crawling across an Aubusson carpet in a navy silk suit, dragging from his mouth a length of yellow ribbon. Behind him, stalking the ribbon and making occasional swats at it, was an enormous gray cat, missing an eye and the tip of an ear, but obviously retired from combat long enough to have become obese. Through his clenched teeth, Gaston Lesseur was issuing directives to the cat, like a coach managing a boxer, balancing encouragement with criticism.

"Mais vraiment," he concluded with exasperation, "il faut faire un petit effort. . . ." It was a phrase she'd often heard her French teacher say to the underachievers. "You must make a little effort," was the more literal translation, but for Lavinia it was the Gallic equivalent of Miss Kaye's admonishment: Bestir yourself! The cat had turned the attention of its one good eye to the close grooming of a paw, splaying its claws like a hand of cards needing to be rearranged.

Lavinia liked Gaston right away; she liked the disorder of his smile, his lower teeth crowding the first one out of line, giving him an unexpected boyishness. She liked the way he had continued his rebuke to the cat even after he had realized she was standing in the room, and she liked that he'd made no effort to explain or apologize for his behavior.

She liked his tie, the hush of elegance in the pattern, and the lazy way it had been knotted. Lavinia had a momentary urge to adjust it where a fold of silk turned awkwardly, revealing its pale underside like a tongue.

"Would you like something to drink? An apéritif? A cigarette perhaps?" he asked, advancing across the room to greet her. The yellow ribbon was bunched in one hand and the other was extended in cordial confusion.

"Do I know you?" was his second question, and "Can I take your coat?" was his third.

"I was told you needed an assistant," Lavinia answered, hastily introducing herself. Even as she said it, it seemed preposterous. It had been months since she'd been given the address by Monsieur Druette and when she found it again in her icebox behind an ancient jar of cornichons, she'd decided to look up the address more out of curiosity and a sense of adventure than the expectation of finding employment.

His eyes registered a flicker of surprise and then he nodded.

"It's very true," he answered in English as he shrugged his shoulders genially and added, "Everyone needs an assistant, n'est-ce pas?"

Lavinia looked around the room at the stodgy Empire furniture, a whisper of dust lacing the outdated grandeur, thin as veiling.

"It looks like you need more than an assistant."

"Indeed," he agreed, "but one must begin somewhere."

"What sort of work would your assistant do?" she asked,

handing him her coat and then her hat. Lavinia had already decided that she wanted the job before she knew what it was. The apartment was overheated and there hung in the curtains the slightly bitter smell of ancient tobacco smoke. Even so, the place had a forlorn beauty she understood.

"No doubt things like hire a housekeeper," Gaston answered. "I don't come here regularly, as you can see. I suppose an assistant would also keep women trimmed in fox fur from appearing unannounced in the library."

Gaston kept talking while he left the room with her coat and wandered down a hallway, and Lavinia wondered if she were supposed to follow him. In his absence, she straightened the seams of her stockings and refreshed her lipstick. When he returned with two glasses of port, she was leaning against the Directoire desk, trying to look relaxed. Her hands, as she reached for the delicate cordial glass, seemed huge and ungainly, and she regretted the alligator shoes she was wearing. They were not comfortable, and the heels, scuffed from getting caught between cobblestones, made her almost as tall as Gaston.

"My wife's uncle," Gaston said, indicating with his head a large portrait behind the desk. "He left us this apartment when he died. I plan to sell it, but first, as his executor, I need to have everything inventoried; Hachette or Drouot will take most of it for auction. And there's more in storage in the bowels of the building. Mostly junk; token offerings Marcel Feydeau, one of the most expensive lawyers in Paris, accepted from clients in lieu of payment. His charity cases were always artists of one brand or another. He must have harbored his own secret ambitions in that direction to have indulged so many drunken deadbeats with oil paint in their hair or clay under their nails. Poor fool was still writing letters to land-lords and prefectures on their behalf long after he retired from practice. The previous concierge used to complain about the bums trudging through the courtyard claiming to have business with Feydeau, deuxième étage.

"How long ago did he die?" Lavinia asked. It was clear that Gaston had been in no rush to probate the estate; the appeal of having a secret hideout was obvious.

"Over a year ago. He died right here, at home. He was seventy-four. No one expected it. Least of all his mistress."

Gaston was smiling as he tipped back his glass to punctu-ate his narrative, draining the last amber sip from the tiny well at the bottom of the fluted glass. Lavinia downed hers as well and when it was empty she held it up to the light to examine it. It was exquisite, the rim of the glass so thin it looked too delicate for use, like the petals it mimicked, the stem no thicker than a stalk of columbine.

"They were Josephine's," Gaston confided. "Or at least that's the family lore. But then all the aristocratic families claim to have something Napoleonic, some keepsake won or earned or stolen, depending on who is telling the story, just as any cathedral worth a pilgrimage has to have a relic. My mother used to say that if all the bones, the fingers and toes and teeth, all the holy relics of the Church were gathered together and assembled, you would have an army."

Lavinia said nothing but held out the diminutive cordial glass, that had once been Josephine's, and let Gaston refill it.

"A believer would say that was just an expression of the miraculous," she said, lifting the glass to her lips, happy to imagine that its gold rim, rubbed over time down to just the memory of splendor, had once been touched by the lips of a woman who had helped shape an empire. It was like kissing history, Lavinia thought tipsily.

"Like the fishes and the loaves?" Gaston laughed, offering her a corner of the sofa he cleared by sweeping all the mail that had been piled there onto the floor. He pulled over a small cane-bottom chair and straddled it backwards, leaning his chin on the top of the back rest.

"I suppose you are very expensive for an assistant," he posited, swirling the port in the glass.

"Yes," Lavinia said.

"Do you have any credentials?" he asked, looking at her crossed legs from the corner of his eye.

"No,"

"Any experience?"

"No."

"References?"

"Only the Consulate."

Gaston grinned, flashing his crooked teeth. "But they are paid to lie. That's their job."

"And I will need to bring my pug," Lavinia added.

"Well, that decides it." He sighed. "You're hired. But only if you agree to brush the cat and always wear that perfume."

Lavinia stood up and brushed the wrinkles from her lap. She was smiling but trying not to smile, as she said, "That's going to cost extra."

"Fortunately, I am a man of means," Monsieur Lesseur replied.

It was almost two months before Lavinia saw Gaston Lesseur again. A large brown envelope had been brought to her door the following day containing a key, a week's salary, a brief note with a list of tasks, and the yellow ribbon.

"The fellow delivering this packet to you is Jean-Marc," the note concluded in a postscript longer than the text: "Don't be afraid of him. He's not fierce, just very slow. He'll come by the Feydeau apartment most afternoons, at around three o'clock, to see if you need assistance. Anything you can find to occupy him would be appreciated. He particularly likes to polish shoes, Consider him *your* assistant, if it pleases you."

Lavinia was baffled; foreign currency always had a slightly unreal quality to it, like play money, but Gaston's stack of freshly minted banknotes, tied with a bow like a pile of love letters, still crisp and bright with printer's ink, looked like loot, or pirate's booty, something from a child's game rather than wages to be earned.

Jean-Marc was also a surprise. Pudgy, with thinning hair and the stoop of someone life has prematurely aged, the only thing Lavinia found even vaguely alarming about him was the sour smell of yeast he exuded. It was clear from looking at him that he was retarded, but not severely so. While Lavinia opened the banker's envelope and examined its contents, Jean-Marc stood stork-like at her door, counting softly to himself while he balanced on one leg, folding the other up behind him and holding it by the ankle until he lost his balance, shifted weight and started again on the other leg. His eyes, hooded and saurian, and his chin shadowed by the need for a shave, or his handful of pointy teeth the color of twine might have lent him an ominous air, but didn't. Even contracted with purpose, concentration squinting his eyes and creasing his brow, his face was gentle.

Lavinia was too taken aback to be anything but charmed by Jean-Marc: that Boswell liked him secured his favor and made it easy for her to find a place for him within her afternoons. By the end of her first week she realized Gaston Lesseur had been right; everybody needed an assistant. When she found nothing else for him to do, she would have Jean-Marc take Boswell for an afternoon walk she choreographed to pass by the post office, the tabac and the bookseller on the Quai Voltaire who kept dog treats in a mason jar under his chair.

Her work on the Feydeau's estate was more absorbing than she had initially anticipated. Lavinia had begun by cataloguing the furniture, room by room, formal to private, and then the paintings, starting with the oils and then gouache, watercolor, prints and finally bric-a-brac while Jean-Marc counted the books, arranging them on the floor in colorful stacks. She supplemented her knowledge of antiques and art with an academic fervor, shaping her free time around lectures on eighteenth-century painting, furniture from the Première République, or the English Regency period. She read essays on forgery, and journals of art criticism. She visited museums and galleries, and familiarized herself with the terms and criteria the critics used to declaim or extoll the decorative arts of the last century and a half.

Those winter afternoons, with the sun slanting low across the floor in burnished bands, jeweled with sparks of dust, filled Lavinia with a sense of happiness so simple and quiet she mistook it for something else. She ascribed the calm bedazzlement that overcame the room to the satisfaction of purpose, and to the light, as if its glow had infused the air with such contentment that it muted sound, reducing the world to the ticking of a mantel clock.

Jean-Marc continued to bring her weekly envelopes from Gaston, in which a note on pale blue stationery always accompanied the packet of banknotes which were always tied up in ribbon, like a present, a colorful millefeuille suggesting something much more festive and playful than money. The notes, written in a large loopy hand, on paper the color of a robin's egg, were an unpredictable assemblage of instructions and thoughts and quotations. Lavinia found herself looking so forward to the notes that the money became increasingly meaningless.

"Please arrange to have the marquetry on the dining room table repaired before it's removed for auction," and "Monsieur Joubert the concierge will come Tuesday to fix the broken shutter," or "The piano needs to be tuned. Let me know what it costs and I'll send a check with Jean-Marc," were the kind of quotidian instructions which might be coupled with a thought about the moss covering the statue of Renée Vivien, the glow of the cobblestones at dusk, or the rank smell of the Seine after rain. Sometimes he would quote a line of poetry from Verlaine or a witticism of Voltaire or a sentence from a book he was reading. Occasionally Gaston would make an inquiry which Lavinia didn't know whether or not to answer:

Dear Mademoiselle Gibbs,

Are you keeping warm this winter? Le Figaro talks about severe cold yet I awake with a damp brow in a room as overheated as the Congo, mistaking the radiator for the rasp of an adder. Have you ever spent any time in the tropics? The heat gets in your blood

*like a fever and surfaces in dreams when you least
expect it. So many things are like that: certain memories, the voice of a childhood friend, an irrational fear,
the refrain of a song you've only heard once or the
scent of a woman's perfume combining orange blos-
soms, jasmine and musk.*

It snowed lightly but repeatedly, dusting the roofs and
rails, smudging the edges of the buildings and erasing the
world on the other side of the Seine. The trees along the river
were hung like chandeliers with ice, their frozen pendants
sparkling like cut glass when they caught the light. The wind,
as it rounded the corner of the Rue Mazarine, whistling up
eddies of snow, sliced like a whip, and the moist air from the
Seine made the cold more penetrating. Nonetheless, Lavinia
found herself walking to work early, Boswell tucked under
her right arm in place of a baguette, and the previous
evening's *Paris Soir* rolled up under the other. She was content to read about the events of the world a day or two late,
but 34, Rue Vaneau, was exerting a pull as powerful as that of
a planet drawing her into its orbit.

There were signs of Gaston in the apartment from time to
time, a wizened end of a cigar, left in a Limoges saucer that
had been commandeered as an ashtray, or an empty decanter
unstoppered on the desk or a bowl of candied almonds by the
bed, and the bedclothes rumpled. Once she found a rabbit's
foot dangling at the end of the yellow ribbon, suspended from

the top of the kitchen door frame with an upholstery tack. Lavinia supposed it was another level of training for the gray cat, like the batting ball at which her brothers used to swing that hung from one of the lower limbs of a sugar maple behind their summer house.

She had begun writing back to her employer, and would arrive at work early to indulge in the pleasure of rereading Gaston's notes before moving on to the even greater pleasure of replying. Her notes would be sent to Gaston via Jean-Marc, who took such evident delight in having the additional commission to perform that Lavinia was able to persuade herself that the correspondence was just part of her job.

Monsieur Lesseur,

I saw the gendarmes being drilled this afternoon in front of Les Invalides. Their boots were so black against the snow and their faces so young I was unexpectedly moved. It reminded me of a haiku I can no longer recall: something about the searing beauty of cherry bark in the rain. For several hours afterwards I felt a terrible sense of grief. Am I going mad?

Sometimes Gaston would respond by embroidering her themes, musing for example on the nature of sanity, the peculiar difficulty of the seventeen-syllable form of poetry, or the sartorial panache of the French uniform. Often too, he would respond obliquely, with just a quotation:

Dear Mademoiselle Gibbs,
   "And time remembered is grief forgotten,
   And frosts are slain and flowers begotten . . ."
            —Swinburne

P.S. Are you feeding your dog my candied almonds?

To which Lavinia replied:

Monsieur Lesseur,
   I see in the papers that the unions are getting noisy again. Do you think I need a raise?

To which Gaston responded:

Mademoiselle Gibbs,
   I think you need better reading matter and to be taken dancing. Unemployment statistics now are so demoralizing we are obliged to celebrate our good fortune at every occasion. I'll have Jean-Marc bring a bottle of champagne tomorrow, Veuve Clicquot Grande Dame, so that you can toast your exceptional luck.

Lavinia understood it as a game involving volley, but not like tennis, with its rapid focus on movement; this more closely resembled badminton, in which there was a sense of elongated time before the satisfying pong of response, setting the shuttlecock in flight on a new path to the same place. In this way, expectation bound the players to each other more surely than any visible tether. It also made possible greater revelation than would have been likely face-to-face.

Gaston sent single sentences, "Thank God 1937 is almost over," and questions, "Is it true that in America you eat the corncobs that we feed our pigs here in France?" He made confessions, "Last night I couldn't sleep so I ate an entire tin of marrons glacés, using the tip of a knife to spear them in to my mouth, which I haven't done since I was fourteen and now I can't think why I waited so long to repeat the pleasure."

He wrote as if he were discovering a language, experimenting with its forms, moving between the hortatory and the interrogatory, between specifics and generalities, playing with inflections and innuendo. His notes, frequent and yet surprising, interwove shards of his life with the tasks he delegated weekly. Much of the work required to probate the estate was dull but Gaston Lesseur's directives, sparked with humor and jeweled with fragments of poetry, became for Lavinia offerings, verbal bouquets which flowered within her.

It was through these exchanges, too, that Lavinia came to know a great many things about her employer. She learned how Delphine, Jean-Marc's mother, had been the cook at his father's home and when Gaston's feuding parents could not agree on which one of them he would visit for school holidays, he would be sent to Normandy, with Delphine and her damaged son, Jean-Marc.

They would stay with Delphine's brother in his cottage

near Etretat which was always damp and cold, but the locus
nonetheless for some of Gaston's fondest childhood memories.
While Delphine canned fruit and cleaned the grimy cottage,
obviously undisturbed by a mop since their last visit, Gaston
would take Jean-Marc for rambles which kept them out until
the light began to fade. They would walk along the cliffs or
down along the shoreline, where the salt from the spray of
breaking waves settled on their clothes and when they licked
their arms they could taste the ocean. Staring out at the horizon, he would let the sound of the surf mesmerize him as he
dreamed of sailing away on any one of the boats that disappeared from view.

Lavinia also came to learn that the name of the gray cat
was Grisette, brought as a kitten to Marcel Feydeau by the
little daughter of one of the artists he helped pro bono. The
story of the cat was complicated, emerging layer by layer, like
a line of music in a score to which instruments in counter-
point continue to be added. The gift had charmed Marcel
Feydeau, so against his better judgment, he kept the animal,
as well as the name the little girl had chosen without knowing
the cat was male. It had amused Feydeau that the little girl
didn't know *grisette* was the term for ladies of questionable
morals. It had been a source of amusement to his family too,
who were relieved that the only "grisette" in Uncle Marcel's
life was hunting mice not men. Monsieur Feydeau had been
unable to intercede successfully on the painter's behalf the

next time he was in trouble, and before an appeal could be filed, the painter hanged himself in jail. Thereafter, Marcel viewed the cat as a reproach and felt obliged to spoil it without ever being able to love it.

Watching Marcel Feydeau interact with his cat, Gaston had come to understand how the same dynamic had informed his own father's relationship with him, and fueled the unhappiness that was expressed in his father's guilty generosity and Gaston's guilty ingratitude. When he realized this, Gaston began to love the cat, and foolishly saw himself in the gray tomcat that would rather fight in the courtyard and on the rooftop with local strays than abide for very long the comforts of a loveless home.

Once, when Lavinia had run out of her perfume, she wore for a few days the eau de toilette she had received as a gift the previous Christmas from her tobacconist. The gift had the unintended consequence of so embarrassing Lavinia that she never returned to the tabac, going two blocks out of her way to make her subsequent purchases on the Boulevard Saint-Michel.

By the end of the week, a bottle of Arpège was left on the mantel in the library with a note:

Dear Mademoiselle Gibbs,
Please remember the terms of your employment, and do not hesitate to inform me when you require supplies necessary for you to continue to perform your duties.

Lavinia was flattered that Gaston had noticed her use of an alternate scent and was delighted by the gift. She had never been given perfume by a man before and it seemed suggestive in an entirely disembodied way. As invisible on the skin as an unacknowledged caress, it left behind just as sure a trace in the memory. She returned with pleasure to her previous scent, noting with satisfaction how much more complex it was than the cloying eau de toilette, which she poured into the bidet, making her water closet reek with girlish innocence for days. By the time Lavinia saw Gaston Lesseur again, she was already in love with him although she didn't know it and would not have admitted it if she did.

The second time Lavinia saw him he was perched precariously on the backrest of an upholstered reading chair, reaching for the chandelier to replace a missing crystal pendant. "You don't inhabit much the nether realm between the earth and sky, like the rest of us, do you, Monsieur Lesseur?" Lavinia asked, as she unpinned her fur hat, trying to supress a smile.

"A man should have range, I think. Don't you agree, Mademoiselle Gibbs," Gaston replied, completing his delicate task before turning smoothly to smile at her. She noticed her heart was racing as she hung up her coat and took her place at the desk, where the dealer estimates and auction contracts were piled, waiting for her to impose order.

Lavinia lit a cigarette and shuffled through some of the

papers, as if looking for one in particular. Because she had her back to the rest of the room, she could not tell if she was being watched, but she was so acutely aware of Gaston's presence, it didn't matter: she felt as exposed as in the dreams in which she suddenly found herself naked at a train station or concert.

She sharpened a pencil self-consciously and corrected her posture. Then Lavinia returned to the folders, selecting one marked *Completed Sales: Receipts*, turning the sheet of paper over with a brisk flick of her wrist, making her bracelets chime as if to testify to her work.

"Mademoiselle Gibbs," Monsieur Lesseur finally said, "please stop tormenting me with your querulous jewelry and tell me if you enjoyed the champagne I sent. It was my last bottle from that year."

Gaston had stretched himself out on the couch, an arm flung behind his head and his stocking feet crossed on the opposing armrest. Grisette padded across the floor and jumped up on to his belly and started purring loudly.

"I did, thank you," she replied, wishing she had thought of something more engaging to say, and wondering if she should thank him for the perfume or if that would ruin the lovely conceit he'd constructed in which it was a necessity not a luxury. He didn't speak again and Lavinia couldn't tell what he was doing, or if, like the cat, he had decided to have an afternoon slumber. When she was able to steal a glance, he appeared to be reading, but Lavinia couldn't be certain he really was.

The Feydeau apartment had begun slowly shedding its contents, so that the rooms seemed to have grown thin over the passing months, like a consumptive wasting away, revealing corners and angles like the jut of increasingly prominent cheekbones. Some rooms, such as the dining room, were entirely empty but for the ornate molding and woodwork, like a stage on which the shifting light made small dramas starring the occasional odd item left in the center of the floor by Jean-Marc or the housekeeper, a wash bucket or pair of polished shoes. Now, from down the long hallway that led to the bedroom, Lavinia could hear, amplified by the emptiness, the crunching of almonds.

"Boswell!" she called out, and there followed the staccato click of his toenails on the wood floor and a head-shaking sneeze as he entered the room, his mouth frothy with the last traces of the masticated white shell of sugar that coated the nuts.

"Oh merde," Gaston said, throwing a hand up in an exaggerated gesture of disgust, "that's why they are so sticky!" Lavinia started laughing, surrendering to a hilarity intensified by the nervous excitement Gaston Lesseur's unexpected presence had fueled.

"Your dog is fired," Gaston said.

"You can't fire him."

"Why not?"

"Because it would hurt his feelings."

Gaston was trying not to laugh, but the corners of his mouth twitched upward in the struggle, making his crooked smile even more crooked and contagious. "I see," he said, watching Boswell circle in the corner before settling down.

"I didn't realize gargoyles were so sensitive. Or had such rarefied diets."

"Yes." Lavinia nodded. "They do."

Gaston left shortly after Jean-Marc arrived, and made no reference to a return. Lavinia was so distracted she put aside the folders and the appraisal reports and flung herself on to the couch that had only just embraced her employer.

For the rest of the day she watched the sky absorb the cold blue of the slate roofs, until only the palest color was left, leaving the world a dull gray interrupted only by the black gleam of chimney pots glossed by a light rain. Boswell settled at her feet and she listened to his sibilant snore as he recovered from his earlier gorge, his swollen belly rising and falling with the slow precision of a bellows. In another apartment somewhere above her and muted by several walls, Lavinia could hear a violin and the same scrap of music practiced over and over again with an urgency that spoke to her agitation, to feeling both replete and full of yearning.

On her way home that evening, under the yellow halo of
street lamps, and dodging between puddles gleaming with a
moiré of motor oil, Lavinia crossed the river to the Right
Bank and wandered into the Galéries Lafayette. For almost
an hour she paced the floors absently fingering merchandise
until she settled on the purchase of a silk slip in a pale shade
of peach and a pair of three-button-length evening gloves,
black with a jazzy red cuff. By the time she entered the passage
way to her building and passed Madame Luberon's check-
point, the open window where her bundled bulk glowered in
even the worst weather, Lavinia already doubted her selections.

The slip was too girlish: it would only accentuate the
flaws evident in her body when she examined it critically
before the standing mirror that dominated her small bathroom. The gloves, removed from the display vitrine in which

their vivid glamour had been as arresting as a hothouse orchid, suddenly seemed like a cheap clamor for attention. The red cuff was too bright, too insistent; garish even.

"Fashion is for shopgirls," her mother had said when Lavinia was young. "Those with good breeding don't insist on the newness of their clothing, or seek to distinguish themselves by their wardrobe. It is taken for granted among the upper class that one will be well dressed, therefore no one genteel needs to crow about it."

The gloves were stuffed in the bottom of a drawer in which Lavinia kept things she almost never used, like the old blanket exhumed only for picnics because it was scratchy, or the flannel leggings she had worn on a ski trip to Austria with Julian Davanne, a beau she'd had briefly the previous year, before she realized she didn't particularly like skiing or Julian either. He had been more sophisticated than Sven and less serious; it had taken only a few months to realize that while he was very entertaining, he was shallow and his words were insubstantial. She had not bothered to save his letters.

The silk slip was put in Boswell's basket and within a day it was stained by a small puddle of yellow vomit that heralded yet another of Boswell's frequent stomach complaints. Lavinia threw the slip away rather than bother to wash it; it had become an unnerving reminder of the disparity between the life she imagined for herself and the one she felt comfortable inhabiting.

Three days later, Gaston Lesseur showed up again at the

apartment on the Rue Vaneau, and after that he began turning up once or twice a week. Often he came late in the afternoon, when the light was beginning to fade and the courtyard slowly filled with the blue weight of evening. By then Jean-Marc was usually gone, though he invariably left behind something as a marker to hold his place against the encroaching night; a tower of books or a piece of half-eaten fruit on the mantel, or a bar of soap cinched at its waist by a red rubber band, or shoes from one of the closets that had not been cleared, staggered across an empty room in drunken steps.

Jean-Marc didn't like to be out in the dark. As soon as the scrim of twilight began to obscure the features on the weathered faces that lined the cornice of the building across the way, he would begin to fret, rocking in increasing agitation and whimpering with a fear for which he had no words and Lavinia had no comfort. The best she could do for him was to make sure he left well before the shadow of night began its blue advance.

Some days, Jean-Marc could feel the press of night well before it was visible and he would hardly stay long enough to take his coat off. His projects were littered around the apartment, always underfoot and waiting for the cat to upset, like anxiety scattered wordlessly throughout the apartment. On overcast days, when the sky was the same leaden gray as the stones of Nôtre-Dame and the waters of the Seine were a dull black, Jean-Marc didn't come at all; the day was not bright enough to lift his self-imposed curfew.

"Don't worry," Gaston had reassured Lavinia. "He's always like this in the dead of winter. There's nothing to do about it. He worries his way to spring. We are all animals at heart," he said, shrugging his shoulders. "And from time to time we also pace like tigers in a zoo. The only difference," and here Gaston paused to light a cigarette, "is that we build our own cages. Jean-Marc's cage, *le pauvre,* is invisible but defined by what is visible. It's very poetic, n'est-ce pas? That he is imprisoned not by bars of light but by their absence?"

Gaston exhaled and the tobacco smoke, like the swirl of his thoughts taking shape, floated lazily along the band of light that divided him from Lavinia on the other side of the room.

"It would be easier on Delphine," he continued, "if he could just hibernate until spring instead of measuring out the winter like a prisoner waiting for a reprieve."

Lavinia hardly noticed the seamless transition by which Gaston's presence began to replace Jean-Marc's. She did notice, however, the way her pulse raced when Gaston was near her, and how if he leaned over her shoulder when she was typing, her fingers became flustered, and how when she was falling asleep at night listening to Boswell's nasal buzz, her thoughts returned to Gaston with the surety of metal to a magnet.

It was not something she generally talked about with her friends. Alice Baker, Anne Aubretton and Lorraine Tyson, the women she was closest to, knew she'd taken a job three days a week, something to do with artworks and inventories. The particulars Lavinia had kept obscure. Work, she'd noticed, whether volunteer or salaried, whether their own or their husbands', was a topic that was generally not pursued by the circle of women with whom she socialized.

"It's work just hearing about work," Mrs. Frobisher said once, complaining of her husband. Lorraine Tyson had pretended to yawn in an exaggerated, silly way and Lavinia had nodded in agreement. At the time she had been assisting Mrs. Aiken with the typing and proofreading for the *Americans Abroad* newsletter, a dull weekly of modest circulation, mimeographed in a tiny office of the Ambassadors Club whose members did not include any diplomats whatsoever, English-speaking or otherwise.

At first, the work at the Feydeau apartment had been just an adventure, something to be savored privately. Later, when Lavinia realized that it was giving her life new shape, igniting an interest in more than just the evolution of modern art or the curves in a Biedermeier chair, she had wanted to tell Alice Baker. Alice was the only one in Paris to whom Lavinia had ever talked in detail about home or matters of the heart. She had told Alice about her broken engagement and about her affair with Sven Larskan. When Sven's letter came that first Christmas, wishing her happy New Year and promising 1937 would be the year Franco was defeated, she'd shown the letter to Alice, who said, "He's obviously still in love," and asked if she could have the stamp.

Alice Baker was also the only friend to see Lavinia cry,

when Elsie Donner wrote in May, saying Sven had been killed in Barcelona. Alice had given back the stamp, pressed between the pages of a book by Lorca.

"It's unbearably romantic, I don't care what you say."

"No, what was tragic was that it wasn't unbearably romantic."

"Still," Alice said wistfully, "it was for him."

"Yes, that's why I had to end it. Even though I liked him very much."

"But now he's dead," Alice whispered, and they had both burst into tears.

The first time that Lavinia had mentioned Gaston to Alice in an animated fashion, sharing some of his quips, imitating a gesture, Alice had clapped her hands and said, "I'm so glad he's not stodgy. I had automatically assumed he'd be stodgy, because the work sounded so tedious, despite your enthusiasm for it." Alice laughed and picked up one of her little dogs. "The way you describe him now he sounds sort of dreamy. I'm imagining a cross between Jean Gabin and Cary Grant, only shorter, naturally, because he's French. What's his name again? Marcel Feydeau? Shall I make inquiries? Is he someone Harold might know?"

"No," Lavinia said, suddenly realizing the awkwardness, "it's not at all likely and really, you mustn't exaggerate. He's no more Jean Gabin than I am Greta Garbo."

If Lavinia was afraid her employer might kiss her, she was more afraid he wouldn't. The irony of this was not lost on her. Gaston Lesseur was the embodiment of all the compromise her mother had dreaded would be forced on her by the Great War. He was Catholic, for starters: he'd been an acolyte as a boy. If she gave any credence to the limp, he was a cripple, at least some of the time. And those were nothing compared to the compromises her mother hadn't anticipated: he was French, and he was married.

"Those poor lost souls," her mother had called the women who had affairs with married men, "condemned to live in perpetual twilight." The tone of her mother's voice conveyed as much pity as contempt for women who would consign themselves to such a limbo. On top of that thorny problem, there

was the distasteful fact that he was her employer. Lavinia
reflected on this at length in the bathtub, where she spent a
large part of her evenings at home, now that the expat community was trickling away, driven home by the falling value of
the dollar and by the increasingly unpleasant presence of fas-
cism throughout Europe. Most of the grand hotels on the
Côte d'Azur had closed. There were tobacco shortages and
the days of walking borzoi in the Bois de Boulogne were over.
If 1937 had failed to be the year that Sven had promised,
1938 was worse. Mrs. Frobisher had been the first to comment on their thinning ranks. "It's hardly worth throwing a
party anymore; you can scarely fill a room with interesting
people these days."

Lavinia didn't miss the dinner parties though, the hired
clairvoyants and the Hungarian pianists, and everybody wanting to have fun in a desperate way that invariably ensured that
no one would. It was hard to go dancing at Maxim's or drinking at the Ritz when *Paris Soir* was full of factories closing
and pensions being cut. Unemployment was high and strikes
and shortages demoralizing: when it wasn't convulsed in
protest, the country felt as if it were in mourning.

"It's too bad you weren't here in the twenties," Lavinia
was told. "What they say is true: there's still scads of bad
behavior now but it's just not as much fun."

It was a relief to Lavinia, not a hardship, to have fewer
engagements that took her away from home now that she
found herself craving solitude for the first time. As her social

world contracted, her secret world expanded. Sometimes Lavinia would stay in the bath long after the water had grown cold, lingering on a phrase Gaston had used, repeating it over and over to herself, or she would remember a look he had given her, charged with meaning, and it would make her stomach skip.

Often she didn't even bother to bring a book into the bath with her. She'd just lie with her head tilted back against the curved rim of the tub, eyes closed, while steam rose from the water. Alice had given her a stack of records for her Magnavox and Lavinia listened to them one after another, wearing out and replacing the record player's needle every few days.

"They're all scratched and Harold left a few on the radiator so those are scratched *and* warped. I was just going to throw them out since giving anything to the staff only encourages stealing."

Lavinia had taken the records gratefully; she didn't mind the scratches. They added a warmth that was comforting, like a fireplace burning green wood, snapping and hissing in the background. If the de la Falaise family who lived above her were away, she would play the records loud enough so that the music seem to vibrate through her flesh down to the bones, where it was absorbed as a temporary anodyne for her ailment. She could no longer deny that she was lovesick. Lavinia conjured Gaston Lesseur in her mind with such constant focus it felt masturbatory whether she touched herself or not.

They continued to exchange notes, which went entirely unacknowledged in each other's presence. He wrote:

Dear Mademoiselle Gibbs,
    Do you think Stendhal was right to use ice as a metaphor for love? The way the café awnings were fringed in icicles this morning it was so magical I was ready to believe anything.

She replied:

Monsieur Lesseur,
    Isn't love already a metaphor?

But there was nothing in their expression or conversation that in any way alluded to the increasingly amorous exchange that traveled back and forth across Paris in the yeasty pocket of Jean-Marc's winter jacket or, increasingly frequently, through the mail. While Lavinia spent the afternoon sorting through bills or organizing the correspondence with the probate court or measuring the legs on a lyre-back chair for inventory, Gaston would read in another room or write letters, or play with the gray cat, making no effort to speak, contriving no excuse to approach her. She wrote:

Monsieur Lesseur,
    Can one die from desire?

He replied:

Mademoiselle Gibbs,
    It is not possible. Otherwise I would have perished
long ago. It is responsible, however, for insomnia, con-
fusion and gray hair.

Occasionally she would look up from her work and catch him standing in a doorway watching her. He usually spoke immediately, as if he had only been waiting to have her attention.

"The apartment will fetch a better price if I have it painted before it goes on the market. Please find out from the concierge whom he would recommend and make the necessary arrangements." In his voice was an unexpressed but unmistakable longing that seeped into the directives he issued, investing them with a sense of urgency and fatigue that gave his words an emotional resonance disconsonant with their meaning. Other times, he would simply look away.

Lavinia fought, not always successfully, the urge to find reasons to address him or simply be in his presence, sharpening a pencil if he were in the study or flushing a clogged fountain pen under the kitchen tap if the dark aroma of coffee brewing located Gaston's presence there. When he helped her on with her overcoat he let his hands rest on her shoulders just a moment or two longer than necessary.

It was at these very moments, though, when Lavinia was close enough to smell the citrus in his cologne, moments when in passing a folder or a coffee cup their skin would accidentally graze and she would feel a surge of desire so intoxicating it seemed worth whatever she might lose if she surrendered to it and entered the shadow world of adultery. It was then that she would invoke the name she least wanted in the room.

"And how is your wife, Monsieur Lesseur? Is she enjoying her stay in the country?"

"It's beautiful there. It would take an act of will not to enjoy it, Mademoiselle Gibbs." He looked up at her, his eyes unflinching.

"Perhaps someday you will see La Rêveline," Gaston continued without pause. "It's been in her family forever but no one uses it much except Céleste, who never seems to get bored there. Everyone else finds the eighteenth-century charm mitigated by the eighteenth-century plumbing. A weekend in hunting season is one thing. A winter there is another entirely."

Shortly thereafter, Lavinia wrote to him:

Monsieur Lesseur,

Is your position at the bank so important or so unimportant that it allows you to spend your afternoons reading Balzac with Grisette?

He replied:

Mademoiselle Gibbs,

I am a man singularly untainted by ambition. That is either my chiefest virtue or my most severe failing. What do you think?

She answered:

Monsieur Lesseur,

I think it is a worthy enough ambition to read Balzac's oeuvre. I imagine it must be a more fulfilling way to pass the afternoon than tidying the temples of Mammon.

Days passed before Lavinia got her reply because a chest cold had incapacited Jean-Marc even more severely than winter's dark undertow. As soon as she had sent her letter, she had worried that she had offended Monsieur Lesseur and that was what accounted for the extended silence that protracted time.

Dear Mademoiselle Gibbs,

How fortunate I am in having an assistant who not only understands me perfectly but is always beautifully attired in the couture of Worth and Molyneux. I am sure you would rather have a raise, but I am giving you a rose instead.

It's a hybrid the almost-blind gardener at La Rêveline has been working on for years, in a hothouse he almost never leaves. One tends to forget he's even there until he suddenly appears with a blossom like this in his hideously clawed hands, ruined by arthritis and Armagnac.

I am counting on its taking your breath away. This strain has a sweet tooth I was told; add a little sugar to the water and it should bloom for more than a handful of days.

Lavinia was so relieved to see Jean-Marc when he returned at the end of the week with the note from Gaston that at first she did not take in how beautiful the rose actually was. When it slowly registered on Lavinia that it was more than just a pretty flower, that it was, indeed, breathtaking, she was grateful that Monsieur Lesseur was not present to see her unravel. She was grateful too that Jean-Marc had hurried off, anxious to beat the retreating light home.

She was able, therefore, to lean over the sink in the kitchen with both faucets blasting water full force into the basin to drown out her sobs. It was the first time in her life she had ever cried from happiness, and she was ashamed by how undone she was.

When she saw Gaston next and he made no allusion to the note, or the rose, or the feelings for which it had been the proxy, Lavinia realized that she would have to make the opening gambit if they were going to have an affair instead of a flirtation. She understood, finally, that his hesitation did not indicate a lack of desire or wavering resolve, or even a moral qualm. Had she not been his employee, or had she not been of his social standing, he might have been more daring. That she was both, however, multiplied the obstacles past the point where he could reasonably assume the inconvenience of his marriage would be surmounted or even temporarily overlooked. It heightened the risk of losing even the circumscribed contact with her that he currently enjoyed.

While Lavinia understood the dilemma, she had no idea how to resolve it. She had never before considered the role of seductress. It had been enough in the past just to have been pursued on a few occasions, by a few worthy men. In a city full of women who seduced with finesse, Lavinia couldn't imagine how to do such a thing without embarrassment, without risking an awkwardness from which they might not recover.

It was a stalemate that kept her up at night, pacing her apartment barefoot, wings of panic beating in her chest. She felt as if she were sixteen again, when everything having to do with love seemed impossible and therefore urgent. She was wishing for a deus ex machina so fervently she almost missed the opportunity when it presented itself. She had written to Gaston:

Monsieur Lesseur,
   Next Thursday is my birthday and I would like to take the day off. The last of the books will be picked up on Monday and there is nothing else currently scheduled for the week. Does your vacation policy include birthdays?

The reply was immediate, arriving the same afternoon. Jean-Marc was splotchy and wheezing from the exertion of having run most of the way. At least, he clarified, as he caught his ragged breath, he'd run all the way from the Pont Neuf. As he handed her the envelope, Jean-Marc beamed. "I ran because he said it was important."

Mademoiselle Gibbs,

It all depends on what your plans are, naturally. If you wanted to go to the zoo, for instance, I'd have to say no. On the other hand, if you were going to be dancing, I'd say yes of course. But then you would need, no doubt, a new dress. Consider it a cadeau from Uncle Marcel. He was a generous man, so splurge. In fact, be squanderous. He would have liked that.

Like a chess move that suddenly becomes obvious, Lavinia understood that if she accepted the gift, albeit one proffered ever so delicately by a dead man, she had all but acquiesced. If she were going to do this, she knew she would need the resolve of a warrior. There was no room for half measures of the heart anymore. Her response raised the ante:

Monsieur Lesseur,

What do you advise? Indigo velvet or claret-colored silk?

All the war metaphors that had always been so odd and alien to her when they appeared in the love poetry she read at Miss Dillwater's for her advanced English class now made sense. The thrill of seduction was in the strategy—and it was more complex and satisfying for some than the pleasure of conquest. Conquest limited its focus on a single moment rather than the elaborate weave of moments in which it was suspended. In seduction, all conversation became a part of the courtship, coloring what would follow. The better the players, the more compelling and subtle the struggle for the lead. Gaston, however, was an expert.

> *Mademoiselle Gibbs,*
> *The obvious answer is both.*

At the club, in a ballroom depressingly underlit and almost empty, Gaston held her, through all the various dances in the band's repertoire, never changing his step, and never loosening his hold. One arm clutched her waist and the other her neck, a hand rising up through her hair to cup her head to his chest. There was no question from the way they held each other that they were lovers or would be soon, their bodies took such obvious relief from the contact.

This was clear even to the busboy who watched them dance from behind the steamy portal in the kitchen door, where uneaten tea sandwiches wilted on polished trays and the Spanish waiters argued about Franco. But it was also clear that they were dancing as if it were the end of a very long evening. There is always a certain resignation or surrender implicit in a conquest, bestowing poignancy in direct proportion to the exertion of the struggle. Even the way they fit their bodies together on the dance floor suggested that the sweetness of fulfillment was tempered by the weariness of a long labor.

This, and the dimness of the light, eroding any distinguishing features of the room, and the diminished numbers of those who had braved the rain to get there, only furthered Lavinia's sense that she had indeed entered a perpetual twilight. It didn't matter though. It was her favorite time of day, and the only one that seemed at all magical. Even as a little girl she had loved its hushed descent, transforming the world into a fleeting dream of beauty and blue shadows, full with unnamed possibility. Verlaine had called it *l'heure exquise*. The exquisite hour. Perhaps, Lavinia reflected, a note of sadness was a necessary component to twilight, the flaw that compromised its beauty, but in doing so gave it a more haunting resonance. She had already learned how longing distorted the very desire it echoed, creating an imaginary distance that no amount of travel could cross.

It had begun to snow by the time he took her to bed. She watched the flakes fall on the skylight overhead, gathering first at the metal edges, and accumulating over the warped glass like the pupil of an eye contracting, until the world elsewhere was shut out, until it was just a pale and distant glow.

Lavinia didn't immediately notice how agitated Madame Luberon had become, that the mail was frequently missorted, and neighbors would tiptoe down the marble stairs at night to slide envelopes under the apartment doors that paired on each landing, rather than brave Madame Luberon about the mix-up. The brass doorknobs and name plates went unpolished and Madame Luberon was no longer waiting until evening to drink.

Olivier, the voluble waiter at the corner café, was talking about Mussolini to any patron who did not actively discourage him. But now Lavinia rarely stopped at the Bacchus for a coffee, except to meet Jean-Marc, to give or receive a letter, and Jean-Marc was equally oblivious. She would go for days without reading a newspaper or listening to the radio, which was full of increasingly alarming BBC broadcasts.

The snow kept falling, and then the rain, muffling the

world, curtaining it off with a gauzy scrim, distancing everything that did not pertain to love. Lavinia's mail had winnowed
with time to just a few staunch correspondents: Dora Fell and
Eliza Hatch, "dropping a line" now and then with news of
their growing families, or a must-read book, sporadic reports
trumpeting a financial triumph, or bemoaning a setback.
Grace sent the bits of gossip she deemed juicy enough to justify the effort of a letter. Her brothers, if they wrote, described
victories: last year, Joe Lewis and War Admiral, this year the
World Series and Don Budge's Grand Slam, and Howard
Hughes circling the world in three days and nineteen hours.

Lavinia now began to let the mail accumulate, leaving it
unopened for weeks at a time. The airmail letters, in their
thin onion-skin envelopes, were from a world even more
remote than the one from which she was now withdrawing.
The pages, delicate as tissue, were giddy with cocktails at the
Stork Club and matinees at the Barrymore, lives on another
continent, in a different universe. In one of Grace's letters
that Lavinia never finished, she had written:

> We saw Orson Welles at El Morocco, and you'll
> never guess who was at his table, wearing a silver
> sequined gown and looking just like a polished can-
> dlestick—Martha Tubman! And she still looks con-
> fused, even all grown up. Even when all she has to do
> is smile. The Sterlings were at Mrs. Drummond's hol-
> iday party, and Shelby's put on weight. It doesn't look

*bad—it makes him look very substantial. A big girth
is all right in a man if there's a big enough fortune to
back it up and now he has that too, thanks to us . . .*

The news from the States seemed especially viscous, like
a syrup: slow to arrive, lacking transparency, and sticky with
implication. The roster of births and deaths, grievances and
gossip had never been much of a tether to her past but now
the letters might as well have been written in a language she
remembered only fleetingly, in a dialect that seemed familiar
but used a different alphabet. The letters made her feel more
detached from the world they invoked, not less. Even
Gordon's letter discussing his wife's death, months after the
event, seemed opaque. He noted that while 1937 had seen
the passing of his dear wife Constance, it had also taken in its
grasp John D. Rockefeller and Andrew Mellon and the race-
horse, Blazing Blue.

It was Gaston's letters for which she paced. Lifting the
wing of the engraved blue envelope was like raising the lid of
a magician's box. She was enchanted; the letters caused a
fever only they could relieve. She would read the words over
and over again, letting them transport her. Certain phrases
rushed through her the way his kisses did, filling her with
longing, making her stomach quiver with a nervous exhilara-
tion she recalled from childhood: the titillation of having
taken a dare, or tipping her head back when the swing

reached its peak, losing gravity in a moment's flight. It was a kind of delirium. She knew that, of course, but it made the sensation no less satisfying. Lavinia wondered if this was what morphine addicts felt, before they had to be shut away or cured.

At first she carried the notes with her, carefully folded back into the envelope on which her name sprawled in his untidy, ragged penmanship. He made even her name look beautiful, slanting in black strokes across the blue stationery, like startled birds filling a patch of sky. Lavinia pressed his words against her skin, tucking them under her garter belt or in her brassiere. It didn't matter if an edge was sharp or a corner rubbed. It was as if Gaston were saying her name, as if his words were speaking directly to her body, as if she could absorb them more completely that way. It didn't matter that it didn't make sense; neither did what she felt.

Dear Mademoiselle Gibbs,

I'm lost. I'm speaking in tongues and all they want to do is kiss you. I think of nothing but when I can see you next. Everything reminds me of you. I am adrift, surrounded by water but dying of thirst.

Last Sunday I went to church, but all I could think about during the sermon was watching your face as you slept. I lit a handful of candles on the way out but didn't say any prayers. I was afraid to mix God up with us, partly because I know you would scoff and partly because I felt too superstitious.

*I need to smell your neck, brush your hair, feel
your skin against my skin. I need to kiss you. Can you
feel my longing crossing Paris to vibrate in the air
around you? I am in the wind embracing you. I am
kissing you even now.*

Once, Lavinia was all the way to the Odéon Métro station before she realized she had left Gaston's note on her
dresser, next to a pair of pearl earrings she had decided not
to wear. Even knowing she would be late for the violin
recital at Madame Aubretton's home in Neuilly, Lavinia
couldn't help herself. She ran back down the narrow streets
to her apartment, her heart racing with panic as if she had
suddenly remembered something left simmering on the
stove.

Dearest Mademoiselle Gibbs,
    *This is ridiculous. I yearn for you like a trem-
bling schoolboy. I tried to read Voltaire and then
Sartre as a cure. No luck, alas. I am now wallowing
in Rimbaud, a beautiful edition bound in red leather.*

Throughout the recital, Lavinia found herself touching
her sleeve to feel that the blue notepaper was still there,
quickening her pulse under her lizard watchband, occupying
the place Miss Kaye had reserved for a sachet of smelling
salts or a handkerchief ready for tears.

Within the first few weeks of their affair, the Feydeau apartment finally sold. They met only a few more times as lovers at 34, Rue Vaneau, before the locks were changed. Now that her job assisting the estate of Marcel Feydeau had concluded, Lavinia realized how much less access to Gaston she had as his mistress than as his employee. They had squandered half a year pining and then no sooner had they become lovers, it seemed, than they were suddenly without a pretext or place to meet. This only fueled their determination, replacing one obstacle with another, adding to the sense of urgency in which desire and destiny seem interchangeable.

Gaston's week still included pockets of time in which he could absent himself from his other life, the work he did at the office, or the work he did at home, which he said was the harder of the two. Without recourse to Marcel Feydeau's home, however, the logistics of a hotel rendezvous made it harder to catch those pockets of time together. Their new relationship precluded the very thing the previous one had afforded: a routine. Only now did Lavinia come to see how domestic their time together had been, occupying a home together several hours a week, season after season. The last time Lavinia saw the Feydeau apartment, it was cold and Gaston arrived late. He had had trouble discouraging Jean-Marc from coming with him.

"He wanted to say good-bye to Grisette," Gaston said grimly as he unpacked delicacies from Fauchon and Delbard, laying out the items in a row along the mantel. He was still wearing his coat and he avoided her eyes as he unwrapped cheeses and slices of ham and *saucisson* from their wax paper.

"I felt like an ogre telling him no. As I was leaving him, he started to weep. I haven't made him cry since I was twelve. Delphine took him to the kitchen, but he kept pleading. 'Why won't you take me with you,' Jean-Marc kept saying. He said it at least four times before he called me a *salaud*. What could I do? I couldn't explain."

"What did you do?"

"I kept walking."

Lavinia drew in her breath but said nothing. The room suddenly seemed more empty. Devoid of furniture, it looked smaller, less distinguished, and the stark light from an unshaded ceiling bulb exposed the absence of everything, even the particular quality of happiness she had known in that room.

Gaston produced a flask and the two cordial glasses that had been Empress Josephine's and poured them each a glass of port. He downed his quickly and poured another right away, filling the glass almost to the rim. He did this before clinking glasses with her, or making a toast, and Lavinia was worried that he might be angry at her. She did not stop worrying until he pushed her up against the wall and she could feel him inside her.

That she didn't always know when she'd see Gaston again left Lavinia slightly off balance, liable to overreact to small frustrations and to anticipate problems that often never materialized. Then, just as she was adjusting to the loss of 34, Rue Vaneau, the bank required Gaston to make several unexpected trips to Bruxelles.

"I can hardly complain," he told her, "since I do so little work as it is; it would be ungrateful not to make a small effort on the rare occasions I'm actually required to do my job."

He had been unbuttoning his shirt while he spoke and Lavinia watched him greedily, marveling that the act of removing his shirt could so stir her, marveling that he could be so sanguine about these impending separations. She wondered if they would have their first fight over it but as soon as his hand was on her waist she forgot how stung she had been by his wording. She remembered only her greed.

My Darling Lavinia,

I'm leaving again for Bruxelles this afternoon, in advance of the directors, who will follow at the end of the week. My only comfort is that I will have several unbroken hours of solitude in a first-class compartment on the train with nothing to do but let my mind ravish you.

For days I have sustained myself on the memory of our visit to Père Lachaise and those last midnight kisses. We should have made love there by the grave of Oscar Wilde with all the stray cats watching; will you ever forgive me?

The letter arrived by mail. Lavinia recognized his blue stationery at once, pale as a robin's egg, trilling among the pile of white envelopes her neighbor held out to her. Madame Braun apologized for not having dropped off the misdirected mail sooner. "I meant to, every time I went out," she said wearily, "but then I would forget."

Lavinia might have rebuked Madame Braun had she not looked so haggard. Under the best of circumstances, Madame Braun was a difficult woman with exacting standards. Too exacting, it was said, for her to ever replace the husband of her youth, lost at the Somme when she was twenty-two. "*Spared,*" was the word some of her less charitable neighbors

used to describe Monsieur Braun's premature departure from
the earthly realms Madame Braun patrolled in her expensive,
pointy shoes.

Madame Braun owned a successful hat shop on the Rue
de Rivoli and she was almost painfully stylish, but not in a way
that made her more attractive. If anything, it made her more
forbidding, reinforcing the effect of her pinched mouth and
wiry hair. Almost everyone in the building, adults and children alike, had been scolded by Madame Braun and when
she was unsure of whom to blame she would leave a note at
the foot of the stairs addressing the thoughtlessness of a
heavy tread late at night or a bicycle left on its side in the
courtyard.

Lavinia had heard from the boulanger about Madame
Braun's cousin who had left Austria with her three children
and whatever could fit in a steamer trunk. All four of them
and the steamer trunk were now occupying Madame Braun's
living room. Madame Luberon had been commenting about
the incessant smell of boiled cabbage coming from the apartment, and Lavinia had seen the de la Falaise children pinch
their noses as they turned the landing.

"It's true. It's true," one of them said, her laughter rising
up the sweep of stairs, "Jews do stink. They really do."

"No," the older girl corrected impatiently, "that's the
smell of Gypsy stew. Jews smell much worse."

Standing wearily at Lavinia's door, Madame Braun still
smelled of perfume sweet with neroli and musk, but there

was a damp spot on the shoulder of her blouse where a baby had drooled, adding to the bouquet of scent the vague intimation of sour milk.

Lavinia looked at the Paris postmark and wondered if the letter had been mailed because Jean-Marc was ill again. His ungainly bulk and coarse features distracted from the fact that his health was surprisingly fragile, and frequently troubled by respiratory ailments. Lavinia had been concerned because it was something he had in common with Boswell and it had been an especially hard winter for the pug.

Since the sale of the Feydeau apartment, Lavinia had seen Jean-Marc only in passing, to hand her a letter and leave. She missed his presence in her day, the comforting sound of him counting whatever was at hand, arranging spoons or matchbooks, the stubby pencils pocked with teeth marks or foreign coins that collected in the back of drawers. She realized how much of a sanctuary the apartment had become in those leisurely afternoons, providing not just a place for the unlikely intersection of their lives, but a reason without which her odd friendship with Jean-Marc felt false.

Gaston was delayed in Bruxelles and Lavinia began to organize her days around the wait for mail in the afternoons. Once in a while she forced herself to go to a matinee with Lorraine Tyson, or to visit Anne Aubretton in Neuilly, or to walk through the Luxembourg Gardens, but mostly she paced in the courtyard, caged until the mailman buzzed the concierge's bell. Like one of Pavlov's dogs, as soon as she

heard Madame Luberon's wood heels clack down the cob-
bled passageway to the building's entrance, Lavinia felt a rush
of excitement. She tried to disguise her eagerness, ashamed
of the ravenous way she wanted to snatch the bundle of letters from Madame Luberon's puffy red hands, chapped and
raw and infuriatingly slow at sorting the envelopes.

Not until she had counted to a hundred, or until she had
attached Boswell's leash to his collar or recited "Ode on a
Grecian Urn" under her breath did Lavinia allow herself to
collect the mail. She made rules and then broke them and
made new rules, half-believing that small sacrifices or particular rituals could somehow bring her a letter from Gaston.

Dearest Lavinia,
   I am useless without you. I had the bellboy find
me Spanish absinthe, but it too was useless.

Answering a letter could take hours. Lavinia had never
written love letters before, nor had she ever received them,
so she worried that there were conventions she didn't know.
She tried to calculate the different degrees of affection that
distinguished *Dearest* from *Darling* and *My Dear* as if there
were a hierarchy and she might overstep herself. Her penmanship was not poor but for the first time she felt embarrassed by its lack of distinction, sometimes copying over a
letter two or three times trying to give her writing some flair.
Often it was only the desire to post the letter on Boswell's

last walk of the day that prompted Lavinia to finally seal the
envelope on whatever draft was currently under her pen.

> *My dear Monsieur Lesseur,*
>   *Please return to Paris. The city has never been so*
> *gray. I'm half inclined to believe you took all the other*
> *colors with you to Bruxelles, along with my heart and all*
> *my resolve. If you can't come soon then write to me until*
> *your hand cramps. I am living from letter to letter.*

No sooner had the letter slid down the dark throat of the
postbox than Lavinia was seized with doubt, chiding herself
over certain phrases or regretting her confessions.

> *Dearest Gaston,*
>   *Two days passed without a letter and I cursed you*
> *and then three letters arrived all at once and I am*
> *speechless. Your words undo me and take all mine*
> *away. I am in full swoon.*

If her letters contained references to the quotidian
aspects of her life, Lavinia worried that Gaston might find
them prosaic, but it was the quotidian that was missing from
what they shared and what increasingly Lavinia coveted.

> *My Darling Gaston,*
>   *Today at the market on the Rue Monge I saw a*
> *man selling mason jars of cigarette stubs. I was quite*

shocked, despite all that has been said about the
shortage. But I know what it's like to need something
so much that pride is besides the point, and the small-
est crumb is worth fighting for. There is nothing I
have that I wouldn't give (with the exception of poor
Boswell) to have you in my arms right now. When will
I see you next? How many hours?

Her questions were often unanswered, left hanging in the
ether like the reverberation of a bell dissolving in the distance, or the responses were delayed past usefulness. It frus-
trated Lavinia that their letters arrived out of sequence and
that they did not necessarily reply to earlier missives.

Chère Mademoiselle Gibbs,
*   I loved what you said about mustard. I love the*
way you sneeze and the mole behind your ear. Do you
have any idea how in love I am? It terrifies me. If I
were with you now I would be kissing your eyelids,
your elbows, the soles of your feet and the small of
your back. I would leave no skin unloved.

Often the letters that were the most stirring were the
ones she most doubted. Sometimes she would turn away
from his words, searching herself for the beauty that he
claimed to see but her eye would find nothing to admire:
large hands and square feet, knuckles swollen like knobby

bamboo, and a profile that was at best severe. It amazed her that Gaston could feel this way about her.

Darling Lavinia,

It's been raining incessantly and somewhere near the bank a sewer has overflowed. It smelled awful, even in the President's office, but of course, no one said a thing. I distracted myself with thoughts of you. I wish I had known you when you were a child. I wish I had been the first to kiss you. I'll be back by the end of the week for certain. Then I'll show you how fiercely I have missed you.

In place of the Feydeau apartment, they met by assignation in a hotel on the Rue Jacob. Hôtel Trois Etoiles was a small, undistinguished establishment whose principal appeal was that no *carte d'identité* was requested at the front desk. Lavinia refrained from asking how Gaston knew about the Hôtel Trois Etoiles; she was aware he'd had other affairs but she didn't want to know the particulars, especially ones of logistics. If she let herself imagine that he had brought other women there, the whole complexion of the place changed, dissolving what little charm it had, leaving only dinginess, and a history of deceit.

The rooms were cramped, barely accommodating the double bed with a horsehair mattress and bedding that looked as if it had never been fresh, not even when new. The wallpaper in most of the rooms was tanned by years of cigarette

smoke, and the carpet, worn thin in paths that led to the bathroom or the bed, held a bitter odor in what little nap was left.

"It's the stink of cheap disinfectant," Gaston had said,
"but I suppose we should be grateful it was used at all."
Lavinia made a point of not complaining, but to her it was the
smell of disappointment, the residue of broken promises and
the ghostly trace of everyone who had sat on the lumpy bed
and felt how inglorious a location for love this was.

It was always the same: she couldn't wait to be there and
then she was depressed by it. Each time Lavinia told herself
that she didn't care if Gaston usually had to leave before they
had time to drowse with their bodies interlocked, talking in
whispers, breathing their words on to each other's skin. But
she did.

Later, she would be flooded with things she had forgotten
to tell him: why she had been late or the dream that woke her
up laughing or the name she had given her rag doll that she
had never told anyone, not even Miss Kaye, or how that
morning a flock of sparrows bursting into flight had looked
just like a gloved hand opening, or how someone had drawn
a swastika in chalk in front of Monsieur Abramowitz's bookstore. There were questions, too, she forgot to ask, such as
where had Gaston lost his virginity or how had his nose been
broken or had he ever smoked opium or when did he stop
believing in God?

She wanted to know which season was Gaston's favorite
and how he had cut his thumb and if he thought Jean-Marc

was drinking too much. She wanted to know if he liked licorice or played an instrument or had ever thought he was about to die. Lavinia wanted him to tell her when he had realized he was in love with her. She wanted to know what he thought of Léon Blum and why Céleste had never had children.

Most of all she wanted enough time with Gaston so that it became a currency she could spend without concern, squander on frivolous subjects if she wished or even in silence, knowing there would always be more. The world was teeming with topics, and Lavinia increasingly chafed under restrictions his marriage imposed on their time together.

Dearest Gaston,

I am delighted that Jean-Marc has reinstated himself as our messenger. It's such a luxury—very Victorian too! I am glad too for the passing contact with Jean-Marc. I've missed him and so has Boswell. It's a comfort to know that even as the shadows lengthen I may still hear from you, or put words en route that will find you before you go to sleep.

Your compatriot Anatole France said that lovers who love truly do not write down their happiness. He was wrong. Lovers who love truly cannot help but write down their happiness. Or unhappiness. I think love compels one to find it a voice. I would write to you every hour if I could. You color everything, are everywhere reflected. A thousand times a day I think,

"I must show him this; I can't wait to tell him that."
There is nothing that is not improved by your pres-
ence or diminished by your absence. Can you blame
me then, for begrudging every other claim on your
time or your heart?

Even Jean-Marc, who follows you like a shadow
when he is not given busywork to occupy his hours.
Even the author who engages your attention before
bed. Or the rose for which you bend in admiration. I
am jealous of the church bells that wake you and the
water you request from your sickbed. Is that folly or
the definition of love?

Lavinia wrote things that she would never have been able
to say: things that were racy and made her blush, things that
Mavis would have called "wonderfully obscene." When she
had first heard Mavis use the phrase it had baffled her. "Isn't
that an oxymoron?" she'd asked. It amazed Lavinia now to
realize there had been a time in her life when she was
uncomfortable saying the word *desire* out loud, even uncou-
pled from any expression of it.

My Darling Gaston,
Sometimes when I am waiting on a line at the post
office or to get my papers stamped at the prefecture,
or even sitting in a crowded bus, I thrill myself by
thinking of you. The faces all around me smile back,
unaware of what I am recalling. How shocked they'd

be to know. This afternoon, I was remembering when you put my hand between your legs and taught me every slang word in French for cock, making me repeat each one until I had the pronunciation just right.

I remain your eager student, practicing my new vocabulary, shaping the words in my mouth, rolling them on my tongue, under my breath. You have such an astonishing effect on me: even the memory of you can make me shiver. If I think of the way you said my name last night my whole body replies. I miss you terribly.

It's absolutely freezing now that the heat is only intermittent. Madame Braun says we are not getting all of our fuel allotment. Boswell does his best to keep me warm at night but it's the thought of you that generates my heat now that the radiator is on strike.

Sometimes when they were lying in bed together Lavinia would run her finger along the dark scar on his thigh, or squeeze the plump pads of his earlobes, trying to memorize all the details of his body, as if knowing which toe was bent or how many freckles he had on his back could somehow mitigate the loneliness she felt in his absence.

"It's like the scar of Odysseus," Lavinia remarked once.

"I don't remember that," Gaston replied with a yawn.

"Yes," Lavinia said emphatically, tracing the smooth dark skin of the scar again. "It was the mark by which he could be

known. That was what was so lovely: Penelope knew him anyway, without it, and of course, so did the dog."

"I didn't know Odysseus played rugby."

Gaston rearranged the pillow behind his head with his
free arm; the other encircled Lavinia's shoulders, holding her
to his chest.

"It was a wild boar, I believe," Lavinia answered lightly,
"not nearly as dangerous," but she was hurt that her reference
to the legendary love story had been so cavalierly dismissed.
She turned on her side and extended her arm to the switch
that controlled the garish wall sconces flanking the bed.
Gaston wrapped himself around her and as she listened to his
breath thicken into the ragged song of sleep she felt a kinship
with all other lovers, but especially Penelope. Only Penelope
knew what it was to live in suspended time, to make a life's
work of waiting.

Gaston's charm was well suited to the task of distracting women from their grievances, but with Lavinia it only exacerbated her unhappiness. The more he delighted her with his presence the more acutely she suffered his absence. His attempts at levity only further inflamed her if she was already feeling aggrieved, and once when Gaston referred to the Hôtel Trois Etoiles as "our unlikely pleasure pavilion" Lavinia laughed aloud; then she slapped him and burst into tears.

"I have become a cliché," she wept. "And I hate clichés."

She wanted to tell him how ironic all of it was, how she was not like this, how in America she had been known for her independence, and for being a good sport. But that too was a cliché. She remembered her mother imitating the Russian émigré society one encountered at Park Avenue parties, saying in a heavy accent that was not particularly Russian, but garnered laughs nonetheless, "In my country, I was king."

Gaston stroked her hair while she wept on his shoulder. Her nose was running and her face was swollen and splotched. Lavinia knew even with a compress soaked in cold water, her eyes would still be puffy by the time they went to dinner at the Bistro Danton, where they frequently dined before parting for their separate homes.

"Lavinia," Gaston said softly into her hair, "please stop crying. You're not a cliché. After all, I'm no longer your boss," he teased, "and besides, at the Bistro Danton they will think I have been beating you."

She laughed again and hiccupped but as she pulled herself off of his shoulder, she noticed the wet smear on his beautifully pressed shirt, like the shimmery trail of a slug.

"You shouldn't make me cry," Lavinia said, as she leaned over the sink in the corner of the room, examining her face in the mirror. "Only beautiful women can afford to look monstrous."

Whatever he said in reply, she didn't hear. The water that had been sputtering and spitting from the mouth of the faucet suddenly gushed into the metal basin with a loud squeal of the pipes and Lavinia plunged her head into the loud rush of water.

●   ●   ●

Over the next several months, Lavinia made a few fleeting attempts to break off the affair, almost always in the heat of anger, canceling any plans they had and forbidding future contact. In response, Gaston wrote with renewed vigor, sending urgent messages with Jean-Marc, as well as by mail.

Ma chère Lavinia,

How can you say I am untrue? My thoughts return to you unerringly, like a homing pigeon. There is no escape. I am in your sphere of influence and I can feel your pull as surely as the force of a heavenly body. Your heavenly body. My new world. Do not banish me yet.

Last night I pined for you, knowing you were at the opera and not with me. I had no right to expect you to be free at the last minute and yet I felt devastated when Jean-Marc returned with your sweet note and I was very annoyed at Alice Baker for having a season box.

I went to my club to mope and drank too much cognac with Antoine Betrillon. Then I argued with his brother about Germany and played a pitiful game of billiards and finally I just went home and listened to my badly scratched recording of The Magic Flute. *I sat in the living room in the dark, listening to Chaliapin and thinking of you. Just knowing we were both hearing the same music made me happier than I'd been all day.*

My Sweet Lavinia,

Do not doubt that I am just as impatient as you for our time together, or that I think of you any less than constantly. If I close my eyes and imagine kissing you my knees become giddy. I lose my balance and sway.

Of course I am greedy for you too, but I am also grateful knowing that the handful of moments I have with you dazzle like jewels in an otherwise barren landscape. I know how you feel about my going to La Rêveline for Easter, when you have only just forgiven me for my desertion at Christmas. Don't you see that one is duty and the other is desire? Doesn't that matter most of all? Doesn't our need for each other warrant suffering the compromises circumstance requires? Is it too high a price for this delirium?

Gaston wrote to Lavinia late at night in his kitchen, covering the white enamel table with pale hydrangea blue notes he scattered like fallen petals in postboxes all over Paris. His letters, some swollen with words and some saying no more than *please*, were posted from various mailboxes he passed on walks or on his way to work, like a gambler who moves repeatedly to different gaming tables to try to improve his luck. Gaston wrote from his club and he wrote from cafés.

Ma Chère Mademoiselle,

When we argue your words sting me for days. I am morose and ill-tempered; even Jean-Marc has been avoiding my company, attaching himself to the guard at the bank and doing chores that keep him out of sight, or staying at home with Delphine. I would avoid me too, if I could.

On the Rue du Panthéon, near the university, someone has painted the street with the Kafka quotation "There is infinite hope but not for us." It made me queasy when I saw it. What use is anything then? I suppose that was the point of the prank but my interpretation was personal not political. I don't know what is served by making us both miserable. Isn't happiness so rare a commodity that we can't afford to question how it comes to us, but just be thankful that it has?

Dearest Mademoiselle Gibbs,

Among the several fortunes my father lost, one involved thoroughbreds. From that fiasco he culled only one piece of wisdom, which he imparted to me in lieu of an inheritance. To master a thoroughbred, he told me, one must tame the spirit without breaking it. That's the first thing most people don't know.

The second thing is that loving a woman is exactly the same. That's why, he said, there are so few great horsemen, or great couples. My father died long before I realized he was right. At the time, I discounted anything he said because he was such an ass. Besides, he was not much of an equestrian and his own marriage had ended in a long and bitter divorce. My response was to avoid spirited horses and smart *women and whenever possible, the complications of love.*

If I occasionally stumble on my way to you, please be kind. This terrifying frenzy of the heart is new to me. I am, after all, just a clumsy stable boy who dreams of one day riding bareback. Have patience. I adore you. Everything we do after the beginning determines the end.

Gaston sent flowers, first in bouquets and then in wicker baskets, crowding the narrow hallway at the foot of the stairs, where Madame Luberon left them in a conspicuous display, inciting Lavinia's neighbors to speculate, whisper and steal. By the time the forsythia began to bloom in the Jardin des Plantes, luxuries were sufficiently rare that many women in Paris were using strands of their own hair to stitch up runs in their stockings. None of her neighbors had the temerity to take a whole bouquet, but few could resist the temptation to thin the abundance by a blossom or two.

Darling Lavinia,

   I was crushed when Jean-Marc returned with no word from you—not even an angry phrase scratched on the back of a torn receipt. He said you were dressed for the evening. Are you trying to make me jealous?

*Isn't your silence enough for me to suffer? If you
won't go back to the hotel at least meet me in a café or
on a street corner. Give me just a few minutes to hold
you, even in your coat. Please give Jean-Marc the
answer I am so anxious to hear. Let me see you.*

Often Lavinia was only waiting for an opportunity to
relent, an excuse for reunion that allowed her to save face.
Depending on the reason for the breach or the duration of
the hiatus, she would make lists of reasons to resume the
affair or reasons to resist. She might call to mind his toenails,
yellowed and cracked like claws, or the wart on his elbow, or
the way his lips tightened in anger, thin as blades and just as
cruel.

She catalogued his failings, his vanities and arrogance.
She thought about the way he puffed out his lips when he was
thinking, and how he always ordered chicken à l'ancienne at
Bistro Danton, with the predictability of a metronome. She
thought of the way his hair smelled after he smoked a cigar
and the clicking sound he made in his sleep or the way his
eyelids drooped if he'd had too much to drink.

Nevertheless, Lavinia almost always weakened in a matter of days.

Dear Monsieur Lesseur,
    *How I hate you for having stolen my peace of
mind. You have stolen my purpose and my pride and*

*yet I love you without proportion. I should add that
you have stolen my will power as well. I'll be waiting
for you at seven at the Bistro Danton.*

Darling Monsieur Lesseur,

    *Yes, I will see you tomorrow. These last few days
have been torture. I haven't slept for more than two
hours at a time. Boswell's got a cough and I can't get
you out of my blood. Just tell me when. I am wretched
without you.*

    *I am undone by the smallest memory. I have only
to remember your words: I adore you. They surge
through my blood like grain alcohol and intoxicate
me. Those words beat in my chest and fill me with an
echo I am compelled to repeat: I adore you. I adore
you. I adore you. Come to me as soon as you can. Tell
me where to meet you.*

Dearest Gaston,

    *It has just started to snow. I can deny you nothing
when it snows. It's so beautiful right now I can almost
forget all the ways I will regret this later. I accept your
invitation but you must promise to never ever correct
my French grammar again, especially irregular verbs.
Especially when I am naked. Stick to pronunciation if
you feel compelled to improve the way I use your language. I'm sorry I threw the gold bangle bracelets at
you but don't ever call me a noisy woman again
because I'm not. I hate this fighting.*

They fought about petty particulars, the tone of a question or a change of plan or a hand dropped too abruptly. They fought in French and they fought in English, about recipes and philosophy and who loved whom more. Always the question of their future hung between them unasked but obvious. It was with them, in the air no matter where they were, like a perpetually arched eyebrow.

It was especially painful to Lavinia that the adulterous nature of her relationship precluded one of the pleasures for which she had so long waited, and which would have made the time without Gaston pass more easily. She resented the silence adultery imposed, and the cruel irony that having finally found a love that inspired expression, she could speak about it with no one but its object.

She had envied the way the other women of her circle, when they gathered for bridge or at luncheons that lingered until cocktail hour, proffered tidbits of their love lives, pulling out details for analysis and advice like shiny baubles to be passed around the table and admired, scraps of an argument discarded like tattered ribbon or a loose button. Lavinia had seen them glow when they were talking about a lover, as if the half-life of love were extended by the secondary experience of recounting it. It was also a bond between the women, tangling them together in an intricate web of confidences.

It had astonished Lavinia that even women who maintained an otherwise impenetrable *froideur* would reveal such intimate things but there seemed to exist an unspoken understanding as binding as a Masonic vow which assured confidentiality. Even Mrs. Frobisher, whose first name Lavinia never knew and would have been uncomfortable using, even Frozen Frobisher, as Alice Baker dubbed her, had anted up. Lorraine Tyson had told them that she knew her husband was having an affair when he started undressing like a prisoner going to the guillotine, meticulously folding his pants over the chair, carefully preserving the crease and flattening the cuff before hanging them over the back of his chair, *consumed with concentration* she said.

"As if a ball of lint was more fascinating than the prospect of our marital bed."

Jacqueline Linnott, whom Lavinia barely knew, told an attentive cluster of ladies at one of Anne Aubretton's luncheons that she had just gotten engaged to a Romanian count. Jacqueline was somehow related to Madame Aubretton's husband, who was a colonel, or to his cousin, who was a nun. Jaqueline had arrived in Paris the previous season with a reputation for being difficult but without the face or fortune that a high spirit usually requires. There had been some gossip among the Embassy circle about Jacqueline because she liked to drink and flirt. Everyone, except the men with whom she flirted, agreed she needed to settle down.

"Emil has a useless title and impeccable manners but no money. And I don't like moustaches. I never have. They're too distracting when you kiss and often they retain the odor of food," Jacqueline said.

Mrs. Frobisher's husband had a moustache but she was silent in his defense. Anne signaled for another bottle of wine to be brought to the table.

"It's funny, because I wasn't even taking his proposal seriously. I thought he was too foreign and too serious. And much too old." Jacqueline's manner, even with women was flirtatious, and her laugh was throaty and suggestive and made everyone feel as if they were having fun. "I told him so and he kissed my hands. Right here in the center of each palm," Jacqueline said, raising up her hands as if his kisses would be apparent, like love's stigmata.

"He told me he would pursue me relentlessly. I just love that word, relentless," Jacqueline elaborated, almost girlishly.

By then her audience was leaning on elbows over the table drawn into a tight knot of attention. They were all half in love with Emil by the time Jacqueline revealed that in the cloakroom at the American Arts Club, behind the last rack of coats, he had given her an orgasm. "Not really! Not in the cloakroom!" Lorraine sputtered.

"Just like that!" Jacqueline said, snapping her fingers in

the air. For a moment no one said anything while she took a drag on her cigarette, enjoying her own bravura. As the smoke streamed out of her tiny nostrils, she added, "Just imagine when we actually take our clothes off." Jacqueline smiled wickedly, adding, "and that's not an asset you lose when the market crashes."

Lavinia often felt a pang of envy, not for the particulars recounted but for the privilege of recounting them. She longed to be able to personalize songs and places, to have, however briefly, a kingdom of two.

Mrs. Frobisher once divulged the astonishing fact that her husband's penis was crooked, which made everyone gasp except Alice, who matter-of-factly asked, "How crooked?" which made the table laugh and tap their wineglasses with their butter knives. But more commonly the material was not sensational, amusing or shocking; its allure was not the lurid. It was the simple and dependable pleasure of romance, almost as satisfying second hand, that made them giddy with questions, eager to savor another taste of love, even vicariously.

Lavinia had often wondered if her friends thought her peculiar for having nothing, ever, to offer. She worried that perhaps they pitied her. The suitors she might have discussed prior to Gaston were by and large men who did not especially interest her so she could not imagine how she would make them of interest to her friends. Moreover the courtships almost never advanced to the point of complication, and seemed to resist anecdote. That there was nothing to say about them was precisely the problem.

Once, because she wanted to have a turn at the table Lavinia had described Monsieur Daumney's attempt to woo her on Bastille Day in the middle of a heat wave her second summer in Paris. He had seated her with great ceremony on the sofa in his aunt's parlor and recited verse of his own composition. It was embarrassingly bad and he was sweating. His bald head glistened with tiny beads which eventually ran down the slope of his forehead and dripped down his face like tears.

Boswell's hacking cough was audible from the corner of the room and it distracted Olivier Daumney. Every time he made a mistake, Olivier would start at the beginning again, each time his voice a little more earnest. The fingers of one hand twitched as if accompanying him on an invisible instrument. At one point, a bead of sweat hung from the tip of his nose but Monsieur Daumney ignored it, and continued his recitation like a long-distance runner making a heartbreaking rush for the last few meters.

It was excruciating to watch. Lavinia dreaded the end of the poem for fear of what would follow but she also dreaded having to hear it yet another time. Across the taut drum of heat that stretched over the city, Lavinia could hear the church bells of Saint-Germain des Prés announcing the elongated hour. Just as the poem came to its ardent conclusion,

Boswell wandered across the room. He sniffed the floor and sneezed, made a beeline for Monsieur Daumney and immediately vomited on his highly polished brown shoes.

The story had gotten a big laugh, but telling it had left Lavinia with a hollow feeling, and after that, she kept quiet about the occasional men in her life whose advances she generally deterred with impenetrable politeness. Those were not the tales she longed to tell. It was the act of loving that was spellbinding, not the act of deflecting it. Without the possibility of fulfillment they were just tedious tales. The stories that always had an audience were the ones that included the word *relentless*.

But even with all the camaraderie and confession that went back and forth between the women, Lavinia knew better than to bring up Gaston. She had not been able to tell even Alice, who left Paris without an inkling of Lavinia's double life. Adultery was a line in the sand that was not crossed. It was a taboo that ran deep, "like cannibalism," Mavis had noted.

If the French were more tolerant, it only made the American and British women less so. They had adopted in France a siege mentality, circling the wagons even closer than usual against raiders. Their condemnation of adultery was so severe it was not even the subject of gossip. It was too awful to mention, like rape, or incest, and shameful in a worse way because it was voluntary, and both parties were implicated.

The only person Lavinia had told of her love before her farewell confession to Harold had been a stranger. Eight months into her affair, Lavinia had accidentally jostled an old woman in the crowded aisle of an open-air market.

"You must be in love or on fire," the old woman said irritably, "to rush through the street like such a fool." It was intended as an insult, but that was not how Lavinia heard it.

"Yes," Lavinia said, turning around. "I'm in love."

The old woman was oblivious, inspecting a clump of beets, so Lavinia said it louder, almost angrily.

"I'm in love. His name is Gaston and you are the only person I've told."

You know sooner or later someone will see us," Lavinia said. They were standing in front of a doorway at 18, Rue du Cherche-Midi, admiring the portal with its rococo cartouche. The architect, Claude Bonnet, had built the Hôtel de Marsilly for himself, in 1738, Gaston informed her. Around the corner, on the Rue de Sèvres, Gaston had pointed out the Société Générale's stone façade which had been reconstructed at the turn of the century. Above the entrance, he showed her the ceramic frieze in which there were five medallions of women's heads, and the continents, named in Latin.

He had wanted to be an architect once, he told her. It was on their walks that he showed her Paris, and because he had studied architecture for three years in his youth, he showed the city to her building by building, occasionally walking her to another arrondissement just to point out a pediment or cornice. They rarely walked together through a garden or the gallery of a museum. When they were in public it was usually only in transit, never at a destination that might have a whiff of assignation.

Sometimes, though, they were careless or cavalier: once, Gaston kissed her in the bright dazzle of daylight, in the middle of the Pont Neuf, and schoolboys had whistled and laughed. Lavinia had laughed too, giddy with what she later referred to as "sunlight kisses." In the back of a Félix Potin grocery store, amid shelves of canned goods, Gaston had kissed her in front of the tins of sardines, and twice in the smoky darkness of the cinema they had kissed.

"Shhht," Gaston said, putting his gloved finger to his lips. "There is nothing noteworthy about stopping here to notice this." He smiled at her, and for that moment she was utterly happy; charmed, as if nothing else mattered but being within the beam of his crooked smile. She marveled at the way he could in an instant make her feel lucky for his love.

"If we paused together in front of just any building," he said, gesticulating dismissively at an undistinguished apartment building further down the block, "such as that insult of banality, perhaps then we would excite comment or suspicion."

"Sometimes I think you want to get caught," Lavinia said, squinting up again at the ornate cartouche.

"Because I am burdened by guilt?" Gaston asked. "I suppose that could explain the action of any Catholic. Or Jew for that matter. It's only the Episcopalians who manage to remain unscathed by guilt."

"*Not* because you feel guilty, though I'm sure you do," Lavinia said, ignoring the wisecrack about Episcopalians, "but for the same reason an escaped convict must dream of getting caught: just to have it over with, for the relief of not having to run or hide or worry anymore."

Gaston would not admit it and it infuriated Lavinia. As they walked against the wind they said nothing, and Gaston pointed out nothing along the way to the Bistro Danton, where in the back room, at a corner table, under a poster of Edith Piaf, she knew he would order, as he always did, chicken à l'ancienne.

"It's true though," Lavinia insisted, after the wine had been poured. Her exasperation was tinged with despair and it welled up inside her the way tears might have at another time. Suddenly she wanted to ruin the evening. She pressed on, driven by the weight of her grievances. They were grievances accumulated over time and honed by sacrifice. Looking at the gleam of grease on Gaston's lower lip, she reminded herself that but for him, she needn't be in France at all, suffering shortages, erratic electricity and political turmoil. All of the hardship and all of the compromise felt like her burden alone.

> *My dearest Lavinia,*
>   *Please try to understand. I know how difficult the situation is for you but don't be unduly angry about your birthday. Céleste did not feel well enough to*

travel. What could I do? I didn't get back from La Rêveline until Monday. I will make up for it a thousandfold, I promise.

Dear Monsieur Lesseur,

How splendid for you that your wife is giving a party on Wednesday. I thought you said you never entertained as a couple anymore. What else do you still do as a couple? Your lies are poisonous. Every time I uncover one it sickens me. No wonder your wife is always ill or away at La Rêveline. Don't waste Jean-Marc's shoe leather anymore. I don't want to hear from you. But do have a ripping time on Wednesday.

She thought of invitations she'd declined when Alice was still in Paris, entertaining on the Embassy's tab, determined to "suck the marrow out of the moment." It had been awkward for Lavinia to be duplicitous about her life, and she hated the way it made her feel cheapened, and it distanced her from her friends. It was lonely being exiled from activities which required a partner and she especially missed dancing. It was isolating keeping secrets: eventually it was just easier to withdraw from situations that required her to deceive either her friends or the earnest bachelors with whom she was paired.

"I have no world but you," Lavinia told Gaston in the first months of their affair. She realized now that when the words ceased to be a metaphor they became a reproach. She drank her wine quickly, taking no pleasure in it, although Gaston had chosen it specifically to please her.

Excepting Jean-Marc, and he didn't count, they had spent time together with no one. There were no witnesses to their relationship, no friends who shared the secret, who could corroborate their love. It left no trace in anyone else's memory. That was the point—to be unseen, like a spy or a criminal, someone whose secret defines them. Someone, she thought, whose secret erases them.

Harold Baker had told her that the Jews in Germany who removed their stars and went underground were called "submarines." She had laughed; it had seemed clever at the time. That was before she had any understanding of what it felt like to hide or be shunned.

As she became intoxicated by the wine, and by the ways she'd been wronged, she felt herself on the verge of dissolving.

"In the end, I'll be invisible," she said a little too loudly.

"What do you mean?" Gaston asked, but his eyes were elsewhere. He was looking for the waiter on the other side of the room. She could see from Gaston's demeanor he found her statement tedious instead of moving and it made her furious. It made her furious too that she knew him so well she could read it in his shoulders, in the set of his mouth, whereas he could not read her at all.

"You never ask me anything," she said.

"You make no sense, my dear. Would you like one of my oysters, or do you just want to pick a fight?"

"Do you never wonder about me? Have you no curiosity at all?" she asked. "Are my parents still alive? Who was my best friend in elementary school? Have I ever stolen anything? What poems do I know by heart? Does it matter to you?"

Lavinia felt herself getting swept away by the riptide of her unhappiness. She began to butter a piece of bread angrily.

"Do I prefer my butter salted or plain?" she asked without waiting for an answer. "Do I hate cinnamon? Do I love strawberries or am I allergic? Am I afraid of spiders? What was the worst punishment meted out to me as a child and why? Did I have a nickname at school? What do I think must be the worst way to die? Because no one else will ever know if you don't."

Suddenly, her anger was spent and all that was left behind was a grief so piercing she had to leave the table abruptly. In the ladies' room, Lavinia ran cold water over her wrists until they were numb and she could no longer feel her heart pounding. She was drunk. She'd realized it as soon as she'd stood up. As she reapplied her lipstick, she examined herself in the mirror. She looked gaunt and the bags under her eyes were more pronounced than usual. "Because no one else will ever know . . ." she said to the mirror in English. In her drunkenness, it seemed the saddest thing you could say.

It was a thought that haunted Lavinia: one ceased to exist by degrees. Near the Place des Vosges she had passed a pile of possessions that had been put out on the street, the detritus of a life heaped on the narrow curb. Most of what remained had been scavenged and scattered, leaving only what was broken or unwanted. Lavinia had stopped on the narrow street, struck by the terrible loneliness of it: packets of letters, soggy with rain, a bicycle basket bent out of shape, clothing too used or out of style to have been taken by passersby.

A few books with damaged bindings were left, a guide to mushrooming from which the illustrations had been torn out, volume R of an encyclopedia, stained intermittently with blue ink. Spilling off the sidewalk, clogging the gutter, were canceled checks and receipts and bills, which had been annotated as paid, *Réglé* written in a delicate, wispy script. It was the handwriting that made Lavinia pause and then bend down to examine it. It seemed so personal, like a tiny voice trying to give meaning to what had become meaningless. She knew it was a woman's hand even before she found the name: Solange Montagnac.

So this was it, Lavinia thought. In the end, this was all that was left. A life could be reduced to an inventory of odds and ends of no particular importance. She thought of Marcel Feydeau and the way she had come to care about a man she didn't know by opening his desk drawer. She remembered the contents because there were so few items, and they were all so poignantly without value to anyone but their owner.

There were a few foreign coins including a buffalo-head nickel, a lizard address book with only three entries, one of which was a candy store on the Rue Fontaine in the 9th arrondissement, nowhere near where he lived. The other two entries had been scratched out so sharply the paper had torn. There was a brass button and a small round tin of lozenges, long emptied but still exuding the ghostly breath of spearmint, in which a small flat black stone had been saved. Two stubs of pencils still bore Marcel Feydeau's teeth marks, and the silver cap to a missing fountain pen rolled noisily in the drawer when it was opened or closed. An envelope, gray from handling, contained a broken watch fob, and several gold stars, of the kind that rewarded the good work of school-children.

Perhaps that's what made Lavinia squat over the debris of

Solange Montagnac and paw through the remnants of her life, to the bafflement of pedestrians. Lavinia didn't even look up to see who remarked rudely that someone in a fur coat did not need to pick through the trash of the less fortunate. It was not clear to her what she was looking for until she found it in a biscuit tin. As soon as Lavinia saw the pink ribbon that bound the contents of the tin together, with a Saint Christopher's medal pinned to the ribbon just at the center of the bow, she knew she'd found Solange Montagnac just as surely as if she had heard, amidst the rubble, a beating heart.

In her hands, Lavinia held the small collection of treasure: a First Communion card, a folded lace handkerchief with the elaborately embroidered monogram *SJM*, a postcard from Juan-les-Pins with the message "Next time will be our time," signed *R* with a flourish. Under the postcard was a telegram announcing a death, an obituary and several photographs.

The top one showed a young couple standing in front of a Ferris wheel. In another, taken in a photography studio advertising itself in gold at the bottom of the cardboard frame, the same young man smiled awkwardly. Attached to the back of the portrait with a paper clip was a canceled Métro ticket and a small passport photo of Solange Montagnac. Lavinia took the picture of Solange because it seemed too painful to put her back on the rubbish pile. Lavinia put the picture in the zippered compartment of her purse, where Solange would be safe.

Lavinia remembered being told by her brother Gordon, when she was still very young, that there was no Father Christmas and no Heaven. She had taken the news about Santa Claus with equanimity: presents arrived under the tree with or without his agency. It was the loss of Heaven that had concerned her. When she asked Miss Kaye about death and what comes after she was told, "You will live on in the memory of those who love you." It had not had the comforting effect intended.

"What if no one loves you? What if those who love you also die?" she'd asked Miss Kaye. "What if they forget or get amnesia?" Lavinia imagined a kind of evaporation occurring in which not only did the person no longer exist but all trace and record disappeared as well. It had so terrified her she'd briefly taken comfort in the notion of Hell because in order to suffer one had to still exist in some sense, and there one certainly had company. Nothingness, on the other hand, was what gave her the nightmares that had required Miss Kaye to sleep in her room on a folding cot. Now as an adult, Lavinia knew that not being known in life was worse than being forgotten after death.

Lavinia my unforgiving darling,

When we fight the world is a miserable place. Do you remember my telling you about Jacques Lucien, the colleague at the bank who married a Scotswoman and learned to play bagpipes? He's been let go.

It was very upsetting. The stenographer wept. On the way out, Jacques kept his head down, like a schoolboy going to the paddle. As he passed me, I saw he was making an enormous effort not to cry. Officially, it was said he'd gotten sloppy with his reports but we all knew it was because he was Jewish. I was on the verge of tears myself. Not just for Jacques Lucien, but for you, and the handful of words you threw at me like daggers.

Lavinia replied immediately, making Jean-Marc wait while she hastily wrote on the back of Gaston's note, so as not to lose even the time it would take to get a sheet of her own stationery and compose a longer response. "Blow on it," she said to Jean-Marc, because the ink had not yet dried when she handed the note back to him. Jean-Marc smiled and began to blow noisily, tiny beads of spittle flying with each puff of breath. "And don't stop for another Ricaud until after you give this to Monsieur Lesseur," she instructed him. He was turning to the door when she reached out her arm to stop him. For a moment she didn't say anything. His eyebrows knit in worry as if he had already done something wrong.

"I've missed you," Lavinia said, straightening his collar. Then she rubbed his cheek with the back of her hand, letting it graze the stubble. He pushed his face into her hand and made a raspy sound that was meant to emulate the purr of Grisette. It had been months since he'd let her do that, and she found herself deeply moved. Dirty, illiterate, and often difficult, he was still the only person in Gaston's life she knew and as such he was the tenuous link connecting their two disparate worlds.

Gaston my sweet,
There are a hundred things I want to tell you tomorrow, but I felt as if I would explode if I didn't at least send you this caress. Je t'adore.

Even with all the things that Gaston didn't know about her that Lavinia felt he should have, there was still so much about her he knew that no one else did. He knew as well what to do with the information he learned, whether it was secret or common knowledge. Others might have known that she loved clementines but no one else would have blindfolded her and fed them to her, out of season, wedge by wedge, between verses he read out loud from the Song of Solomon until she was intoxicated with pure pleasure.

Sometimes Lavinia asked Gaston about the other lovers he'd had during the course of his marriage to Céleste, but it was never of the mistresses that Lavinia was jealous. There had been three and they had all been married women. When Lavinia asked why, he said, "Because married women are discreet, grateful and gone." Only one had lasted any length of time.

They had been chosen specifically so as not to threaten the marriage but merely provide occasional relief from it. The tales he told about them were amusing and it was clear from the way he discussed them that the genial affection he felt for them now was emblematic of what he felt for them then. Their claims had never been on his heart, nor had any of them wished to complicate an otherwise satisfying arrangement.

Only Danielle Davidot had endured, despite the fact that

Gaston found her mind prosaic and her couture pedestrian. "No flair, anywhere," he said, waving his hand in the air dismissively, but the sex was dependably good, and she was pleasant company. Didi thought of herself as a freethinker and had been in "analysis" for several years with a Swiss doctor who had studied with Freud. The stories about Didi had always been the most humorous, often making Lavinia laugh aloud. Her favorite anecdote was the one in which Gaston took Didi to La Rêveline while Céleste was on the Riviera with her mother, and Didi's husband was traveling on business.

The couple had spent an illicit night together in the master bedroom. Because the plumbing at La Rêveline was famously bad, being both noisy and ineffective, Didi had tried to pee sitting on the sink. She had only just begun to relax when the ancient fixture pulled away from the wall and crashed onto the tile floor. When Gaston opened the door without knocking, he found Didi sitting on the floor, beside the two halves of the porcelain sink. Her mouth was open in shock, and a broken pipe sprayed her with water, as if she were the statue in a garden fountain.

"Not a French garden, il faut dire," Gaston added, "because French gardens are never silly, even when they are trying to be."

Lavinia had been amused when she heard the story but it was Gaston's imitation, his eyes bulging and his mouth open in the shape of shocked modesty, that made her snort with laughter. Later, Gaston would assume the comic mask to make her laugh when other gambits had failed. It became a gag between them and while it continued to amuse Lavinia every time, she also noticed how lazy it was. But by then the prism through which she viewed Gaston had already developed cracks.

His failings did not shift from minor to major arcana until Lavinia learned that Danielle was also a friend of Céleste's, and that Gaston had known her prior to his marriage. This was the first dose of irreparable disillusionment Lavinia choked down like a bitter tonic. It made her previous complaints, that he sucked air through his teeth when he was concentrating or walked half a beat in front of her on the sidewalk, seem endearing by comparison.

It was not Danielle's adulterous liaison with Gaston that Lavinia found repellent; Lavinia was not a hypocrite nor was she a moralist: it was Danielle's relationship with Céleste that offended Lavinia. Didi, as she was called affectionately, by both husband and wife, never felt uncomfortable socializing with the unwitting Céleste, or Didi's equally oblivious husband. That Gaston had involved himself with someone Céleste knew and trusted, *someone she entertained in her home*, disturbed Lavinia deeply. She was shocked by it, and Lavinia had come to think of herself as being shock-proof. That the situation was merely the construct of convenience rather than the heart's command only increased the distastefulness.

It was the first time too that Lavinia felt sorry for

Céleste—protective even. There was something obscene in the thought of the two couples dining out together at Le Grand Véfour or Tour d'Argent, making small trips to charming places, letting Céleste collect happy memories at her own expense. To Lavinia, it was the difference between infidelity and betrayal. It spoke of a moral corruption that was the difference between a gentleman and a bounder. For the first time she questioned Gaston's character.

Lavinia thought with a sickening pang of her eldest brother, Ambrose. As the eldest of the siblings, he had always liked to calibrate the distinctions between wrongs, and negotiate apologies or bribes accordingly, and now as an adult he did so professionally, as a judge. "The world abounds with bounders," he liked to say with a harsh laugh. "There's low, and then there are the rungs below."

It was confusing to feel sorry for Céleste after having suffered such jealousy because of her. Much as Lavinia had fought against it, the passion with which she had come to envy Céleste had been powerful, and demeaning. Lavinia never suspected, however, that it had also bound them together just as surely as it cleft them apart, or that she would come to feel compassion for Céleste for many of the same reasons that had initially inspired contempt.

The ruthlessness with which Gaston had betrayed Céleste by sleeping with her friend, so casually, for so long, suggested to Lavinia something much more complicated than just infidelity.

"In all of Paris, you couldn't find a woman to amuse you who didn't share your wife's affection and trust? Does Céleste have so many friends that she can afford your turning one into a traitor?" Lavinia demanded. The betrayal had in it a kind of cruelty that was particularly difficult to justify because it was so gratuitous.

If Gaston had been compelled by love or even spite, Lavinia would have been better able to understand, but this was laziness, and arrogance.

A line from a Gilbert and Sullivan song came to mind: "A man whose allegiance is ruled by expedience . . ." and Lavinia had trouble banishing it. Her ability to trust Gaston was the linchpin on which her sacrifice depended, and her ability to admire and respect him was what her love required not to wither. Lavinia remembered Mavis talking about the way to choose a lover as they rode a crowded Madison Avenue bus together.

"The body is an instrument capable of expressing both the heart and the soul. But without either engaged, sooner or later the pleasures of the flesh are bound to disappoint, no matter how priapic the performance. Any relationship is only as limited as its participants. Sex with anyone less than an equal is just opportunistic and unsatisfying. Better to have sex with yourself. At least that won't lead to regret or disease."

Lavinia had been embarrassed by Mavis's candor and volume, and later, when Lavinia looked up *priapic* in the dictionary, she had blushed. Mavis had been in her own unconventional and uncouth way more honest and moral than almost anyone else Lavinia had known, and suddenly she wished fiercely for the friendship she had been relieved to let lapse years before.

There had been a time when even hearing Céleste's name had caused Lavinia's stomach to knot and yet she'd been helpless before her driving desire to know everything she could about her rival. Céleste, she learned, had been selected like a piece of furniture or a draft animal, not for aesthetic reasons but for sturdiness and temperament. Céleste had been chosen to breed: she was sweet and simple and a virgin. Gaston could make the word *sweet* sound like a disease and at other times he used the adjective in a way that was tender and painful to hear.

Gaston had become bored by Céleste; he freely admitted it. In bed and in conversation she had never held his attention the way even Didi had, but he loved her nonetheless and couldn't bear to hurt her.

"Céleste not only goes to church, she fervently believes. Divorce would kill her." The more Gaston talked about his marriage, the more it came to resemble in Lavinia's mind her relationship with Boswell. Lavinia knew how compelling devotion could be. Regardless of the source, it yielded a kind of loyalty that almost nothing could replace.

There had been times when Gaston had been tempted to leave Céleste, times when Gaston's sense of claustrophobia in her presence had almost driven him to decamp. But he had never been able to go through with it. "It would have destroyed her," he said repeatedly, but Lavinia suspected otherwise. Alice Baker, who donated generously to a British organization formed for the protection of animals, had told Lavinia that animals caged too long would not leave the cage even when the door to the cage was left open.

In fact, many of the chimpanzees shrieked with fear and clung to the bars of their cage when rescuers tried to liberate them. "It becomes all they know and trust; they become their own jailers. If freedom comes too late it's no longer recognized or wanted. They won't save themselves even when they have the chance."

The fact that Céleste had been so easy to deceive seemed sad. It began to erode Lavinia's happiness to know that it depended on the humiliation of another. Gaston saw it merely as convenient. "What she doesn't know doesn't harm her" Gaston argued, and Lavinia wondered if Gaston had also used that reasoning to deceive her.

Looking back in hindsight, Lavinia was amazed that she'd ever been jealous of Céleste, ever wished for what she had. Once when Gaston was getting dressed, Lavinia had noticed his sock had been darned clumsily at the heel and she'd felt a searing pang that it was not the work of her hand. Alone at night she had tormented herself cataloguing things Céleste took for granted that Lavinia would never have. No matter where the list began, it always ended with his name, and privileges it accorded.

At the Hôtel Trois Etoiles, Lavinia and Gaston had registered as Monsieur and Madame Verdurin, borrowing the
name from a particularly unlikable pair in Proust's long opus.
It had been an amusing nom d'affaire, but even so Lavinia
had felt a frisson of pleasure when the desk clerk addressed
her as Madame Verdurin because it conferred the only recog-
nition of their couplehood she had known. It did not convey
the respect she would have had, however, as Madame
Lesseur, a fact made obvious every time she endured the desk
clerk's snickering "Enjoy your stay," when they checked in or
the prurient titters of the porter when they checked out,
"Come again, do come again."

Gaston justified his infidelity by blaming it on Céleste:
"The nuns ruined her. Only two years with the Carmelites
and she's incapable of having an orgasm. The girls had to
shower in their slips. They were forbidden to look at their
own naked bodies. It's not a surprise Céleste has no interest
in sex." He shrugged and lit a cigarette as he continued his
rationale. "I understand. I sympathize, but what about me?
Our marriage would have suffered far worse had I not made
my own arrangements."

"So you're doing her a favor by being with me?" Lavinia
asked angrily.

"Damn it, Lavinia, if I wanted you any more I'd spontaneously combust. This is why I shouldn't tell you anything at
all. It only upsets you and you use it against me. You're angry

if I don't tell you about Céleste and you are angry if I do. It's a stalemate from which there is no escape." Gaston suddenly started laughing.

Lavinia looked at him quizzically, finding no humor in his sophistry.

"Stalemate, don't you get it?" he repeated, reaching for the ashtray to stub out his cigarette. "The pun is in English no less."

When she got home from that encounter she was still angry. She had raged at behavior that was beneath the man she loved. It made her think less of Gaston when he spoke of his wife with condescension or contempt, but it infuriated her that even so, he still put Céleste's comfort before her own. She wrote to him that night, letting her words pile up into drifts of outrage and supplication that obscured the original shape of her thought and distorted the message. She hated him for disappointing her and she hated herself for wanting him no less even as he diminished in her eyes.

Lavinia wrote to him as if somehow finding the right words would change things; like a magic formula, like the name Rumplestiltskin or olly olly oxen free. She wrote with a desperation that was new and then she stopped abruptly. Lavinia refused to see Gaston and maintained a long and painful silence. It was like fasting, requiring more and more resolve with each additional day. It was a different kind of starvation but it had the same withering effect. Her silence lasted almost a month during which his letters came in sporadic bursts, like the shouts of a swimmer caught in an undertow and losing wind.

Lavinia Ma Belle,

If you are going to end this won't you at least do it to my face? Don't you owe me at least that? I have things to tell you that can only be whispered. Let me kiss you with words. Let me at least cover you with phrases of desire and regret.

Dear Lavinia,

If only you could think of someone besides yourself. Do you have any idea what it was like to have to go back to the Prefecture for another interview? And without a complete set of the documents for my military exemption in my portfolio? Without your love in my breast? You make it hard to be a stableboy much less a hero.

Chère Lavinia,

Tonight the streets of Paris are empty and the mist has swallowed everything, like a world evaporating as I watch. I too, might evaporate if I were not so swollen with grief. Why must you be so cruel? Do you take pleasure in making me suffer? Why did you leave my gift unopened? You might as well have left an ice pick in my back and a corkscrew in my heart.

Lavinia my sweet,

Did you see the full moon hanging over Paris last night? It seemed to balance for a while on the spire of Saint Eustace, as if it had been snagged there. I thought of you and hoped you were also looking up. It was too beautiful not to share. I ached for you then and I ache still. Don't you have any words left? Aucun mots? Même pas un seul?

When Jean-Marc rang her bell with an envelope in hand he was more and more often drunk. Madame Luberon complained to Lavinia about it, and Lavinia agreed that in future, if Jean-Marc was visibly drunk, Madame Luberon would not admit him to the courtyard. Lavinia didn't bother to argue, even though she knew Jean-Marc would not understand why he was no longer being admitted at the door and it would certainly hurt his feelings.

Lavinia might have argued with Madame Luberon, whose own inebriation was increasingly frequent, but Lavinia had noticed that coincident with his drinking, Jean-Marc's hygiene had deteriorated to an alarming degree, making the sharp bite of pastis on his breath almost welcome. He no longer shifted from foot to foot, probably because his balance was impaired by alcohol. Instead, he hunched forward and rocked while he counted, but it was clearly joyless and without comfort.

Now, without his childlike charm, Jean-Marc seemed

threatening in his lurching movements, and unsavory. His eyes were vacant and rimmed in red and it gave his face a haunted look, as if he had just done something unspeakable. It was only a matter of time until there would be a problem with the neighbors. The Germans had made everyone edgy.

Lavinia had seen a man get his jaw broken in front of one of the market stalls at Les Halles over whether Bois Roussel, the French upstart winner of the previous year's Derby, could outrun the lead cyclist of the Tour de France. She missed Alice, and Boswell had developed a tremor in one of his back legs. The papers talked about stolen coupon books, bribery and the black market. No one, it seemed, was at his best and resentments ran like static electricity between people having even the slightest interactions.

Madame Braun had spat at Madame de la Falaise as the final punctuation of a loud and ugly exchange, amplified by the acoustics of the courtyard so that everyone with windows on the interior was scalded by it. It was wearying, like unrelenting rain, or the oppression of great heat. Jean-Marc was not a battle she wanted to add to a landscape already fraught with skirmishes and filled with mines.

Dear Monsieur Lesseur,

Share your sensitive observations of nature with your wife next time you feel a spasm of conscience. I am exhausted by a happiness predicated on my ability

to pretend either you are not married or I don't care.
I am thin from living on the scraps from Céleste's
table.

After she sent that note to Gaston, she stopped responding to his missives for several days. When Jean-Marc returned
at the end of the week with instructions "to collect an envelope for Monsieur Lesseur," his jacket was seasoned with
sawdust and smelled of vomit. Lavinia was reminded angrily
of Gaston's rude remarks about Boswell's nervous stomach.
"Just a minute," she said to Jean-Marc as he stood in the
doorway. When she returned, she gave Jean-Marc an envelope enclosing a blank sheet of paper. It was a cruel gesture
and she knew it, and it gave her a sickening satisfaction.

During the days in which her contact with Gaston was suspended, Lavinia wandered the streets without aim or pleasure. Like a kite released into the air, she felt untethered from the world, but it brought no sense of freedom; she had never felt so restless or trapped. Her walks were too much for Boswell, who tired easily and panted even when at rest, so she stopped bringing him with her. Lavinia walked a random course through Paris until she was exhausted and her feet were cramping.

It occurred to her once, as she sat in the back of a café and wiped the blood from her heel, where a blister had broken, that she was behaving like a penitent. And I didn't even spend an hour with the Carmelites, she thought, with bitter amusement. When the waiter came for her order she asked for a cognac, drinking for the first time by herself in public.

The heavy smoke of cheap black tobacco hung across the room in layers mapping the currents of air. It was a depressing room that someone had tried to brighten with orange curtains. The panels of cloth were hemmed unevenly and seemed to tilt toward the bar, as if imitating the disheveled clientele standing in the front room. A street musician wandered in and began to play a song on his out-of-tune accordion but the waiter waved him off before he had completed the first chord change.

As Lavinia sipped her drink, she smoked the last two cigarettes in the cigarette case Gaston had given her. It was one of the only presents he had given her that she liked; it was simple and there was nothing about it that suggested "mistress" the way the red satin mules with marabou did or the silk peignoir. Often his presents had embarrassed her. The undergarments were tarty and the mules pinched at the toe.

Even watered down by the establishment to a pale amber, the alcohol had a rapid effect. A poem suddenly began to bloom in her as the heat of the liquor spread through her in a tingling rush. Lavinia took Gaston's most recent letter out of her handbag and on the back of the pale blue paper she began to compose the first and only sonnet she had ever written. It took several drafts to complete, and another cognac.

While she wrote, a man with wavy auburn hair and bad skin sat down next to her and rolled two cigarettes. He was almost good-looking, and Lavinia could see in the sudden brightness of his match that his hair was a source of vanity, and from the way he shook the match to extinguish it, he clearly fancied himself a ladies' man. He was drunk and he was complimentary, marveling at her with a smoothness that was practiced and yet stirring.

Over the course of an hour she accepted his cigarettes but otherwise ignored his attentions. She was revising the poem, still astonished to have found it swelling in her, like an unsuspected pregnancy.

> *Sometimes in these words I find*
> *A peace that elsewhere*
> *Flees a fevered mind,*
> *And lifts the shadow of despair:*
> *He loved me well for a brief while*
> *And taught my body how to smile.*
> *No matter that it couldn't last*
> *Or left me wounded all alone*
> *Caught between the pretty past*
> *And a future full of sand and stone.*
> *Send him back now to his wife,*
> *And let him live his other life.*
> *I will learn to love again—*
> *The only question just is when.*

The man murmured something Lavinia didn't hear and then he put his hand on her knee. He had moved closer and she became aware of the warmth of his body; his hand felt like it was radiating heat. When at last Lavinia looked up she saw instantly his flaw. His features were pleasant if bland, but his eyes were little, much too little for his face, giving it a porcine quality despite his slender frame. He looked particularly pink and piggy when he smiled.

Lavinia turned quickly away from his leer and from the corner of her eye she saw herself in the mirror behind the bar as a stranger might. It was a reflection that was brutally unflattering and it sobered her. This is just what my family feared I would come to, Lavinia thought.

"What you have in mind is simply not possible," Lavinia said firmly, removing the man's hand. Now, as she stood above him, pulling on her astrakhan jacket she felt a surge of tenderness replace disgust. A lock of his beautiful auburn hair had fallen across his brow and he was looking up with hurt confusion, a finger nervously playing with the St. Patrick's medal dangling on his chest. She took a last drag on the cigarette and rubbed it out on the corner of an ashtray they had filled during his brief courtship.

She had smoked four of his cigarettes, rolled in one hand and licked closed with a suggestive flick of his tongue. Lavinia understood now that the cigarettes were a kind of kiss by proxy, allowing him to place his saliva on her lips while establishing his entitlement to considerations. Disgust rose up again like bile in her throat. His mouth was weak, and there was something cringing about the set of his shoulders, as if all his swagger could not conceal a crippling cowardice. She was struck by how much she preferred the cruelty of Gaston's lips.

Lavinia thought of Gaston again, and his kisses. For a moment she faltered, her legs wobbling slightly under her as she considered the possibility that she might never kiss Gaston again. As she reached out to a greasy table to steady herself, soiling her glove in the act, she felt the weight of eyes on her back and thought: those men at the bar think I'm drunk. They think it's the alcohol that has made me lose my balance. But it's much worse: it's the memory of a kiss.

Lavinia took a taxi home and reviewed in her mind the poem. The rhyme of *while* and *smile* was clumsy and she decided the use of the sonnet form was schoolgirlish. All of it was embarrassing, even the impulse behind it. As soon as she was home, even before she took Boswell out for his last walk, she put Gaston's letters in the sink and burned them. It was harder to get the envelopes to light than she had imagined it would be but she kept striking matches until the smoke yielded to flame. The paper edged itself in the thin scalloped line of flame, curling up the corners, fluttering as if the words were trying to escape.

It was painful to watch and twice she was tempted to reach into the flames to rescue what was left. Her eyes were tearing from the sharp bite of the smoke but she was undeterred. Lavinia added her poem to the fire and watched her handwriting erased a few lines at a time. When Lavinia had been a child, Miss Kaye had told her about the Spanish conquistadors wading ashore to the New World while their ships burned behind them.

"Why would they burn their own ships?" she'd asked Miss Kaye incredulously. Miss Kaye was sitting in the kitchen eating toast slathered with marmite sent to her in monthly packages from Ireland. "So there's no going back," Miss Kaye said, looking down at the toast. "Nothing fortifies one's commitment to the future as much as eliminating the past."

Lavinia opened the kitchen window to let the room air out. A few black flakes of ash stirred and tried to rise. Even Miss Kaye had been wrong, Lavinia realized. There was no way to eliminate the past. The best you could do was eliminate its souvenirs.

Two days later when Lavinia saw Gaston, it was by happenstance. He was dining in the restaurant where Anne Aubretton was celebrating her saint's day with a handful of friends. It was his laugh Lavinia first recognized. It pierced her like an invisible arrow, drawing in her breath and making her drop her napkin. When she spotted him, he was at a table in the corner with four men in tailcoats. They had come from something formal or were going on to it. It didn't matter; either way there was suddenly no air in the room. She looked away immediately but she could feel his eyes searing her.

Lavinia excused herself and as she left the table, she was so pale Madame Aubretton whispered to her niece to stop eating the mussels. Lavinia was almost at the door to the ladies' room when she felt the hand at her back pushing her on past the washrooms, his breath at her neck. At the swinging door to the kitchen he stepped in front of her and led her roughly through the kitchen, like a gendarme making an arrest. The kitchen crew looked away, busied themselves with tasks, not wanting to know what they might be witness to at a time when nothing was innocent anymore. Into the alley, clattering through tins emptied of olive oil and duck fat, waiting for the metal collection, Gaston pushed Lavinia in the direction of the deepest shadows.

There he kissed her, wrapping himself around her, pulling her underwear down, his hands everywhere on her skin. The way they kissed was like divers coming up for air, gasping for each other as if the only way to breathe was through the other's mouth. Then his fly was open and he bent her back against a wooden barrel without saying a word, making her moan.

Before he let go of her, he tipped Lavinia's head back and kissed her again, but it was tinged by the sadness of what went unsaid between them, by the irrefutable eloquence of their unbroken silence.

As she hurried through the kitchen, careful to meet no eyes, she could feel him leaking out of her and she tightened her thighs instinctively. From the start of the affair, Lavinia had not worried about pregnancy. It had seemed beside the point, like worrying about seating on a lifeboat. Don't play at the high-stakes table, Gordon had told her, unless you are prepared to bet the bank. Lavinia couldn't remember what

Gordon had been referring to, since no one in her family liked gaming, but her love was important enough, she reasoned, that she could hang her future on it. Sometimes she saw it with an almost religious clarity: she could put everything on red 21 and not lose either way.

"Goodness gracious," Madame Aubretton said, when Lavinia returned to the table. "We have to get you home right away—I just knew there was something wrong with the mussels. You look feverish, my dear, so no need to pretend you haven't taken sick. I've already called for the car."

By the time Lavinia saw the surprise of bruises on her back and thighs she was too tired to be shocked. She stared at herself as she turned sideways to the mirror, astonished that the night had written such an alarming message in her flesh and she had been oblivious. Each of her vertebrae had been rubbed bright where it had pressed against the rim of the wooden barrel. There was something beautiful about it as well as disconcerting; her spine had become a string of rubies glowing against the white of her skin, highlighting her backbone, exclaiming both its strength and its frailty.

As she fell asleep that night Lavinia saw how severely she had miscalculated the degree of difference between deliverance and damnation. It had been hubris to think that she could find an equilibrium in an inherently unequal situation, to balance the hours of delight with the days of desolation. It seemed particularly naïve to have believed that the object of a great love must necessarily be worthy of it, or that she could trust the pull of her body to choose the right direction for her life.

Lavinia wondered why it surprised her to find that one could love someone long after one ceased to like them, or that the heart, like the body, could snag on a bramble that only dug deeper the more one tried to shake free. It was a thought that would return to her with the force of a blow, months later when she saw a pigeon caught on the barbed wire lacing the Hôtel Lutetia, where the Gestapo set up headquarters.

She remembered Mavis saying in a barely credible Brooklyn accent, "When it comes to love, you never get what you pay for. . . ." and it had always made Lavinia smile. At the time Lavinia had thought Mavis was a cynic but now she saw how innocent Mavis actually had been. The problem wasn't that love might be overpriced; it was that it could bankrupt you. It could take as much as you had, down to your last breath.

In all the literature Lavinia had read at school, the message had been clear: love was not for the squeamish. When she tried to think of an exception, nothing came to mind. She was sure there were exceptions, but she couldn't think of a single one. Lavinia wondered how she had missed it, written her papers on the use of simile, or classical allusions, ignoring the larger caveat, as if employing a fop to do the work of the warrior.

But Lavinia was practical; if there was no turning back

then she would press forward. She wrote to Gaston immediately, without any further illusions about her ability to stop
seeing him.

> *Dearest Gaston,*
>
> *I can still smell you on my skin. I can still feel you
> inside me. There were times last week, during the end-
> less rain when I would have welcomed the worst exco-
> riation just to hear your voice. Let's kiss until we can't
> remember why we used our mouths for anything else.
> I have longed for such little things—to feel your fin-
> gers laced with mine, or smell your cologne.*

In September of 1939, when communication with America was cut off, Lavinia felt powerless for the first time in her life. Great Britain, France and Poland had effectively stopped all telephone service between New York and Europe following Hitler's invasion of Poland. Even exchanges between diplomatic representatives and their home governments were restricted and, in England, severed.

Now it meant nothing to be a Gibbs. Harold had tried to warn her but the Gibbs family had been so steeped in privilege that Lavinia had been unable to imagine circumstances beyond which her family could prevail: they knew everyone; they were people for whom exceptions were made. Even abroad, even in banishment, even with the forfeiture of status and its attendant perquisites, she had enjoyed the psychological comfort of connections if not the material comfort of them.

Her family had been in Washington and Wall Street for so long they had acquired the kind of power that creates its own prestige. Nothing was ever too much further than a favor someone could do, no matter how loath one was to ask it, no matter what obligations or encumbrances it implied. That was the unspoken safety net she'd taken for granted; that was what she lost when connections were cut off.

It didn't matter with whom she'd danced at which Christmas party or sat next to at which event. It didn't matter that her father knew Jean-Jules Jusserand, who had been the French ambassador in Washington for twenty-two years and close with Teddy Roosevelt. Her father would delight dinner guests with the story of how Jusserand and Roosevelt swam naked across the Potomac, except the Frenchman kept on his gloves, "in case we meet a lady." None of that mattered now. Now she was nothing more than a metic, a Greek term the French had borrowed to express their xenophobia, and designate aliens with no rights. Fate had burned her ships, investing her love for Gaston with even greater value.

War is a great leveler, Ambrose had said on the only occasion he spoke of his participation in the Great War. His tour of duty had been brief, no more than ten months, but it had taken almost twice as long for him to be all right again. At the time, Lavinia had assumed Ambrose's comment was personal, an explanation for his breakdown. It was in keeping with her mother's terse assessment, "The more brittle, the more easily broken," and her father's comment, "There is no shame in life knocking you down as long as you get up again."

Within the first few days of war it was obvious to Lavinia that Ambrose had meant something else entirely: he'd meant that war, like weather, spits on all men alike, and erases temporarily even the distinctions men make among men. It was a powerful thought, not only because it made her feel a deeper affinity for Ambrose, but because she knew that the sense of camaraderie that bound together everyone in an air raid shelter was rare and fleeting and came at a terrible price. It was an irony that Lavinia relished in the huddled damp cellar of her building, sharing a blanket with Madame Luberon on her right and Madame de la Falaise on her left.

There was something exhilarating too about feeling *needed* as opposed to just useful. Lavinia's days were not just full, they were worthy. At first, she worked with Mrs. Frobisher and Lorraine Tyson, coordinating the English Speaking League and several church organizations. Lavinia's efficiency was quickly noted and she was plucked from the haphazard crews of volunteers to work with Mrs. Aiken, a ruddy-faced Brit, at the Croix Rouge.

Because Lavinia was practical and organized and made decisions quickly, she was given what seemed to her undeserved responsibility. Often the work she did was tedious, but she felt ennobled by it. It mattered. The only other thing that had made her feel that way had been her love for Gaston.

Now each reinforced the importance of the other. Mr. Gibbs had warned his children about the dangers of gambling. There comes a moment, he said, when a player starts to feel so much is at stake he can't fold no matter how bad a hand is dealt. "Married to the kitty," her father called it. As a little girl it had sounded lovely to Lavinia to be married to a kitty, like something from a fairy tale.

It was no longer possible for Lavinia to receive bank drafts, which had been among the difficulties Harold had foreseen in his warning. In addition to the money she had in her checking account, she had savings, enough for close to a year if she was frugal. Before the dollar dipped, her father's stipend had been sufficient to allow her to live comfortably and still save at the end of each month, which she had done with Gibbsian discipline in the hope of eventually buying an apartment.

She also had the salary she'd earned working for the Feydeau estate in the five and a half months when Gaston was still her employer, before he became her lover. Lavinia had never spent the packets of banknotes he'd sent tied up in the yellow ribbon of pastry boxes. She had put the money, uncounted, in a hatbox, where she had also kept his letters until she burned them, a gesture she now regretted with wincing frequency.

It was at night that Lavinia was frightened. Even before curfew, the streets were empty, and darkness, when it came, was complete. Sounds seemed magnified; the low rumble of propellers in the distance was enough to know what kind of plane would pass, and how soon and whether or not it was a Stuka. Fear had acquired a new vocabulary. Alone in bed, her heart galloped long after the shriek of the siren had passed, and Lavinia sometimes would get up and put her coat on over her nightgown and sit, Boswell in her lap, on the landing of the stairs, where she could hear the muffled sound of coughing coming from Monsieur Vedrian's apartment and the creak of Madame Braun's floorboards when she paced. It was comforting in the darkness, and helped calm her enough to go back to sleep.

Céleste took ill again and retreated to La Rêveline, taking her cadre of servants with her. Paris was emptying and shops were closing; only a handful of bus lines were still running and it was no longer possible to get the blond tobacco Lavinia liked, not even on the black market. Mrs. Aiken told Lavinia that so many children had gotten lost or separated from their parents in the rushed flights depleting villages and clogging roads, the Croix Rouge had been asked to assist. "How do you lose a child?" Lavinia asked. "How do you lose thousands and thousands?" Mrs. Aiken corrected.

At the Gare Saint-Lazare, while Mrs. Aiken tried to find the supply of typewriter ribbons that was supposed to have arrived, Lavinia tried not to stare at the wounded being unloaded from the trains. Gaston was neither wounded nor away; his military exemption (Lavinia assumed it had to do with his limp) and his wife's extended absence had made it possible to return to a more domestic arrangement. When Céleste regained her health and one by one, inexorably, the servants left, she talked of rejoining Gaston in Paris. "Paris is no place for you now," Gaston told Céleste.

For the first time in almost a year, Lavinia and Gaston had a routine again, and it gave her a sense of security that seemed to make up for the rest of the world unraveling. Since the beginning of the war, they'd met in an apartment on which Gaston's bank had foreclosed. Gaston had copied the key for Lavinia, and just to be able to unlock the door behind which he waited had added an authenticity to their ersatz life together in which she basked.

Before Gaston left for La Rêveline to visit Céleste, he'd kissed Lavinia's nose, saying, "I'll be back, I promise. The only thing in the world I want is here," he'd said. He'd given her an extra coupon book and a liter of olive oil, things scavenged from vacated apartments that had made their way to the black market. It wasn't even considered stealing: it was thrift, letting no resource be wasted. "Take care of Paris till I get back," he'd told her. "I'm leaving you in charge."

Lavinia looked at one of the boys on the platform who had paused to adjust his crutches. His head was bandaged in white gauze, like a turban, jeweled with a bright red ruby improperly centered. His lips were trembling and a bead of blood leaked down his forehead from under the bandage. It made

Lavinia queasy to watch it. Only the night before she had told Gaston, "I have never been more in love. Despite everything. Right now, this very second, I've never been more full."

If war imposed its own constraints, it also allowed them less rushed time together, intensifying the sense of abandon with which they met and the sense of abandonment after they parted.

Lilacs were still in bloom when the German Panzers crossed Metz. Lavinia could feel the press of panic in the air, like the choke of pollen when the plane trees come into flower, making it hard to breathe. It was primitive, instinctual, an awareness of vulnerability an animal has even in its sleep. It was akin to the claustrophobic feeling she had when she wore her gas mask during drills, but, unlike the mask, there was no way to remove it. The roads were thick with the last wave of people heading away from the approaching army.

Along the embankments were scattered items that had become too heavy or cumbersome to complete the journey. Left in the grass or by a ditch, familiar objects were jarringly out of place and took on a forlorn, disconcerting quality. Mrs. Aiken remarked that it reminded her of the work of Tristan Tzara, the Dadaist, whom she'd met once at a *vernissage,* and he had not been wearing any socks. To Lavinia, there was something heartbreaking about the objects and painfully intimate. These were the things people couldn't leave behind, which made it all the more terrible when they did. Lavinia didn't say anything though: it seemed wrong to be moved by abandoned bric-a-brac when men were dying in fields farther north.

Lavinia was also with Mrs. Aiken when she saw the old woman in the wheelbarrow. They were returning from the airfield at Le Bourget, riding in the back of a military transport vehicle Mrs. Aiken had arranged to take them as far as the banlieu. Shutting her eyes in the sun, it felt to Lavinia almost like a hayride, bumping along a back road, with the wind on her face.

"What a glorious day," Mrs. Aiken volunteered. "If I didn't know better, I'd say it was 'a day for lingering and love.' That was the expression we used growing up," she added, with a blush, "for days like this. Ones that make you want to be lazy and foolish."

As they sped around a turn, their driver honked and swerved, jostling them off balance. Receding behind them they could see an old man steering a teetery wheelbarrow through the dust they left in their wake. The wheelbarrow was rusted but it had been lined with a quilt and pillow and looked like a prehistoric perambulator, containing in its belly the slump of a tiny old woman with some belongings piled on her lap.

"Now there's love for you," Mrs. Aiken said. Lavinia nod-ded but she was thinking about the haunted expression frozen on the old woman's face. It was a face in which were reflected all those cast-off treasures they'd had passed along the road, the miscellany of things too precious to leave, but, ultimately, too heavy to carry. The old woman looked as if she were doing the calculation of her weight and his love and the distance they could cover before she too was left in the shade on a grassy shoulder of a secondary road.

After Dunkirk, Cinzano no longer advertised itself as the optimist's drink, or took care to specify its French fabrication. Italy declared war on France and the Germans bombed Paris. The 15th and 16th arrondissements and Auteuil were hit, as well as the airports at Le Bourget and Orly. There was an acrid smell of smoke in the air and it permeated everything: Lavinia's clothes, her hair, her dreams.

"It's the stink of defeat," the baker said when he gave Lavinia her bread ration. "You can't see it yet. But you can smell it," he said, tapping the side of his nose with a finger smudged with flour. "And you can feel it here," he said, indicating his liver. Within two weeks, German troops entered Paris.

Lavinia listened to de Gaulle's broadcast from London at Mrs. Aiken's apartment, sitting on a scratchy divan with a pair of Siamese cats and a woman named Thérèse, who cried softly, wiping tears from her face with the back of her hand.

"She'd been like that for days," Mrs. Aiken told Lavinia in the kitchen. "Since Dunkirk. She doesn't understand how lucky she is that her family's boat was too small to help in the evacuation. Still, you have to admire her for wanting to go."

The kitchen was filthy and as she talked, Mrs. Aiken killed a cockroach, mashing him against the counter with a dirty plate. "I'm never here," she explained, gesturing at the mess. There were people, Lavinia realized, who found their genius at the very times most others lost their way. Mrs. Aiken was like an Olympic athlete for whom the work of a lifetime was compressed into a brief and noble struggle. It was hard to imagine her going back to the tedium of the life from which she claimed to have sprung.

Mrs. Aiken opened a tin of imported shortbread cookies she'd obviously been hoarding. "If General de Gaulle couldn't stem her tears, maybe these will." Mrs. Aiken was not someone Lavinia would have befriended under other circumstances but months of war had made Lavinia appreciate her. Barbara Aiken did not go to pieces no matter what. She reminded Lavinia of home at a time when it was hard not to be homesick.

Lavinia wondered if Gaston had heard the speech. He was out of town at La Rêveline and had been away for the bombing. Lavinia alternated between being grateful he was safe and feeling he should have been with her.

Like love, war elongated time and then compressed it. It

had its own logic and rules. Occupation, Lavinia discovered, was just a debased version of war: all of the privation with none of the sense of purpose or hope. It brought out extremes. Adversity didn't create character, Lavinia saw; it revealed it, like sycamore trees, Lavinia thought, when the bark was peeled away, exposing the trunk beneath, stark and vulnerable. She understood too how it happened that someone became a person you could no longer recognize. It happened incrementally, while you were looking elsewhere, focusing on something other than the lights going out, bulb by bulb, until suddenly you were in the dark.

"Just because someone betrays you doesn't mean they don't love you," Madame Luberon said. She had been crying and her face was striated with the wobbly lines of tears darkened by eyeliner. "Everything gives under pressure," Madame Luberon said, her voice raw, stripped of emotion. She held a bouquet of twigs in one hand and bent to collect others the wind had scattered across the courtyard.

"It's just a question of how much pressure and how it's applied," Madame Luberon insisted, snapping a twig to demonstrate.

Madame Luberon leaned her face so close Lavinia could see the shadow of a moustache above Madame Luberon's lip.

"Humans are no different," she continued in a ragged voice. "And it has nothing to do with love, believe me. If the choice is between sentiment and survival, sentiment becomes a luxury. Just like that," she said, snapping her swollen fingers. Her eyes welled up with tears as she turned away. "Everything gives under enough pressure. It's a law of nature," Madame Luberon repeated.

Lavinia learned from her neighbor, Monsieur Vedrian, that Martin Luberon had spent the weekend at the Hôtel Lutetia, where the Gestapo had set up headquarters. After two days of "room service," Martin Luberon had informed on his twin brother, Michel, who ran a small counterfeit operation selling ration cards and transit permits, with a sideline in smuggled hams.

Upon release, Monsieur Luberon had gone directly to the Pont Royal, and jumped. Lavinia was aghast. It was a terrible story in a hundred ways. It was also the first time the war had touched someone she knew. The war had not just permeated her world; it had entered her home.

"What a waste," Monsieur Vedrian added, and then he leaned away from Lavinia and spat vigorously into the street. Most people had lost weight since the war began, but Monsieur Vedrian looked particularly shrunken. His collar gaped at the neck and Lavinia could see his Adam's apple bobbing vigorously under the stubble on his stringy neck. It made him look fiercer, like an old rooster, angry eyes and a scrappy demeanor puffing up the last few feathers.

"Luberon should have taken a few Nazis with him if he was heading for Hell," the old man said. "Still, I admire him for the counterfeiting. I thought he was just a lout. Just goes to show you never know about people."

"But I thought it was his brother who was doing the counterfeiting," Lavinia said. Monsieur Vedrian rolled his eyes at her innocence and exhaled a dismissive puff of air from his pouted lips, "They were like this," he replied forcefully, twisting one knobby finger over the other, "so I can assure you he was involved somehow, even if he was just the brawn."

For a seemingly endless handful of nights, Madame Luberon wailed and ranted, drunk and beyond comfort, throwing breakables into the courtyard, snarling at anyone who tried to help. No one, however, called out for quiet in the dark courtyard. No one complained on the stairwell. The circumstances were so deeply disquieting that Madame Luberon's loud anguish was a relief from the inevitable reflections that were otherwise disturbing the building's sleep.

Then, abruptly, Madame Luberon stopped keening. She cut her hair with pinking shears and let the gray show; she stopped wearing housedresses, stopped drawing the seam of an imaginary stocking down the back of her leg with eyebrow pencil the way other women did to keep up an appearance. She started wearing her husband's clothes, and continued to discourse on the laws of nature and the nature of betrayal but her delivery was dispassionate, almost academic.

Madame Luberon became fastidious about the care of the building, polishing the ornate brass sconces that flanked the stairwell or scouring the paving stones in the entranceway, or repainting the numbers on the apartment doors with black ink. But there was nothing apologetic about her behavior. If anything, she seemed more fearsome, as if anger and grief had only invigorated her. Madame Luberon still smiled when she saw Boswell though, and insulted him affectionately.

When sugar was rationed, Lavinia left her first allotment outside Madame Luberon's door. By the time Lavinia collected her second allotment, however, she had become more circumspect about her altruism; 750 grams of sugar was too precious to bestow like that, no matter how satisfying the gesture.

*M*y *Dearest Gaston,*

Jean-Marc is looking more and more derelict. Yesterday he had a black eye. Isn't there anything you or Delphine can do? There must be a better way to keep him out of trouble and out of bars than using him as our messenger, which no longer has the Dickensian charm it had before he started drinking all the time. Please don't be annoyed with me for mentioning this, or being so hypocritical as to send it with Jean-Marc. I didn't want to sully our evening later. The more precarious things become everywhere else, the more precious our time together, and the more fiercely I want to protect it.

For her birthday they met at La Mère Catherine, behind the Basilique du Sacré Coeur, for a dinner neither of them could eat. Lavinia had never been to the restaurant before, though she'd heard of it. It dated back to the French Revolution. Sven had told her about the words Danton had scrawled across its wall: BUVONS ET MANGEONS, CAR DEMAIN NOUS MOURRONS. "Let's eat and drink for tomorrow we will die." Staring glumly at the motto that had been a magnet for tourists in better days, Lavinia thought about what had brought her to this: the eve of her fortieth birthday, in an occupied city, in a foreign country, without family or fortune, with a married man who sometimes seemed to love no one but himself.

There was not much on the menu; all the good cuts of meat, all the good anything, went to the Germans. Lavinia ordered pot-au-feu and thought about what Gaston had said earlier in the evening in a brief but bitter skirmish between them, the cause of which was already forgotten. "You do not have a sufficiently nuanced view of the truth," he had insisted. She had accused him of being an opportunist and he had replied, "Throughout history great men have always been opportunists. As an American of privilege I would have thought you'd noticed."

They were both on edge and Lavinia drank half a carafe of house wine before she relaxed enough to tell him what she'd heard from Anne Aubretton whose husband, Col. Aubretton, had just returned from Angers. He'd been among those who accompanied Count Metterich, head of the German army's artistic conservation unit, to the depository in Brissac, where the treasures of the Louvre had been moved for safe-keeping during the war. Metterich had been persuaded to supply adequate coal to ensure heat for the artwork that would otherwise be damaged by a hard winter. Lists had been made too, of châteaux, which by virtue of artistic merit or historic value would not be occupied by German forces.

"I'm sure that will comfort the old and ill who will freeze to death this winter while they keep the statues warm," Gaston had said bitterly.

Lavinia ignored him and continued.

"He also told Anne that internment camps were being built all over France. It's very organized, apparently. Different camps for Communists, and Jews and prisoners of war, and even ladies like me, foreign nationals. 'Tea bags' we were called, lumping all the English-speaking women together." Lavinia paused, and took a sip of wine. She had been looking at Gaston while she spoke, noticing how drawn his face had become in the last few months. As he poured more wine for her from a carafe on the table, she avoided his eyes and continued.

"Anne thinks I should go to stay with Clarissa Dobbs Duvallet. I've never met her but she used to work at the *Herald Tribune* and she's rumored to be taking in strays. Her husband was killed in Dunkirk and she's taken her little boy to his grandparents' charterhouse, in the Auvergne. It has a history going back to the revolution of being 'commodious' in times of trouble."

Gaston took her hand in his and examined it, as if looking for the answer there, instead of in her eyes. "What did you tell her?" he asked, tracing with his finger the pale half-moons of her nails.

"I said I had compelling reasons to stay in Paris for as long as I could." Lavinia looked at Gaston, who brought her hand to his lips and kissed it, but neither of them smiled.

It was raining the day Gaston told her he was a Jew. Beads of water streaked the window and a small cascade spurted from a crack in the gutter. Lavinia kept her eyes at the window for a long time. It was the first time he'd come to her home, though after the war began she'd often suggested it.

"I'm not *really* Jewish," Gaston explained. "I was raised as a Catholic by my father and for better or worse that's what I believe, when I believe. My mother was Jewish, but she didn't practice. She didn't like religion of any variety including Catholicism. 'The world's my temple,' she'd say, 'and observation is not limited to Sundays.'

"When my parents divorced, she moved back to England and then to the sanitarium from which she never emerged. By then she'd lost a lung and most of the will to live. My memories of her are troubled and sad. That my mother came from a Jewish family never featured in my view of her. Or of myself. It wasn't important to either of us."

As Lavinia watched the rain erase a child's chalk drawing from the courtyard, it seemed as if Gaston's voice were washing away their past with the same weary detachment. His words fell steadily, blurring everything, dissolving what was true. They pounded out everything else. She didn't care that he was a Jew; she cared that he had lied. It was almost like vertigo the way the revelation swept her off balance. All the times he could have told her rushed to her temples and pounded in her ears.

Lavinia wondered if it was a failure of feeling or trust on his part that had excluded her from his secret, though both were painful. She wondered what other secrets he had kept from her and the thought made her feel hollow and sweaty. All the time she had been endeavoring so vigorously to be known, he had been equally exerting himself to remain unknown.

She remembered holding hands in the warm darkness of the cinema, watching the Pathe newsreels, hiding together from the usher's flashlight: safe from all the world. All that footage mocked her now: the reels showing the broken storefronts in Berlin, armbands on overcoats, swastikas painted on temple doors, all that time, thinking she had been his only secret. She remembered his anecdote about the American named Robert Kahn who had been turned down at Gaston's club. At the committee meeting, the club president had said, "There will be no Kahns at this club, unless the first name is Genghis." She thought back to their conversation about Léon Blum, and Dreyfus and Céline's *Ecole des Cadavers*. Lavinia remembered the day Poland was invaded and Gaston had quoted Proust, "Pacifism sometimes multiplies wars." Looking back, there had been so many occasions for candor and now those memories were tainted by its absence.

Everything they had together was a secret predicated on a lie. Did he even love her or had she been just as much of a fool as Céleste? A poem long forgotten returned to her in a broken rush. She couldn't remember the title, or its opening line. She couldn't remember the author, or even most of the verses, but she remembered its devastating conclusion:

> *Ah, love, let us be true*
> *To one another! For the world, which seems*
> *To lie before us like a land of dreams,*
> *So various, so beautiful, so new,*
> *Hath really neither joy, nor love, nor light,*
> *Nor certitude, nor peace, nor help for pain;*
> *And here we are as on a darkling plain*
> *Swept with confused alarms of struggle and*
> *   flight,*
> *Where ignorant armies clash by night.*

It was either Longfellow or Arnold. Shelby Sterling would know; he would probably be able to recite the poem in its entirety, Lavinia reflected fondly. Even so, Shelby had lacked the passion to be true on the darkling plain. Now, that was all that mattered. It was the only thing she had thought she could count on.

As the import of Gaston's words registered, Lavinia realized her left hand was so tightly clenched her nails were cutting into her palm. Now nothing was sure. Nothing was safe, not even their love.

All afternoon it rained, bringing down the last leaves of autumn, and banging the loose shutter on the apartment Madame Braun hadn't occupied since the end of August, when, according to the terms of the Armistice, refugees were returned to Hitler. Madame Braun had chosen to go with her sister and the children, one hand holding a baby on her hip, the other carrying a red alligator train case.

"I have a French passport," she'd explained. "I'll come back once I've gotten things straightened out." Lavinia had watched the group of them file across the courtyard, accompanied by two gendarmes, one of whom helped to carry some of the luggage. Madame Braun was wearing a hat with a spray of black feathers and very bright lipstick. She had looked stylish again, as if she were on her way to something very chic and sophisticated. When Madame Braun turned for a final glance at the courtyard, Lavinia waved to her from the window. Madame Braun's hands were full so she couldn't wave back, but her shutter, banging against the window, had been waving good-bye all fall.

The rain was letting up, changing octaves as it drummed the rooftops, and plinked against the copper flashing on the eaves. It was getting chilly and Lavinia pulled the window closed and sighed.

"It could be worse," Gaston said, with forced levity. "I could be a Nazi." The darkness of the afternoon was melting into evening, turning the windowpane into a mirror reflecting Lavinia's face back into the room.

"Sweetheart," he said, "I didn't realize it would be a problem until the prefectures were asked to supply all the records of births and marriage registrations. Even then, I was sure I could find a way."

"Because for you exceptions are made?" Lavinia asked, recognizing the familiar fallacy. It was the one on which she had been raised.

"Because I am not some dirty Gypsy beggar. I'm a French citizen with standing. Because I am Catholic, damn it."

"No," Lavinia said, angrily. "According to Nazi law, you are a *Mischling ersten Grades*." As she spoke she watched her breath fog the window, the heat of her words making the world momentarily opaque. It was a term she'd first seen in an editorial in *Le Figaro*. Harold had explained it to her. Hybrid first degree: the offspring of an Aryan father and a Jewess mother. Until 1934, Hitler had allowed them to keep their jobs provided the Aryan father was still alive. Later, no consideration at all was made for their paternity.

"Think of it this way," Harold had elaborated, "Louisiana may distinguish all the degrees of negritude from mulatto to octaroon but when it comes to intermarriage there is no gray: just black and white, and never the twain shall meet."

Lavinia turned from the window; her heart was fluttering in her chest. Boswell pawed at her legs and whined, wanting to be taken out. The afternoon had vanished and twilight was falling.

"I have never felt so utterly alone," she said. "And all I have ever wanted was to be with you."

In the days following Gaston's disclosure, Lavinia noticed that shop windows displaying signs excluding Jews now seemed to be everywhere.

"Isn't it enough," Lavinia had asked at their parting, as she dried her tears with the back of her hand, "that I have to worry about my own safety without now having to worry about yours too?" Since she'd learned his secret, she'd done little else: new regulations under the Statut des Juifs restricted work to only certain jobs, and then in quotas. No business ownership, partnership, or civil service was permitted now. The current definition of a Jew, and this had been a subject of animated debate in several newspapers, was someone with three Jewish grandparents, or two Jewish grandparents, if also married to a Jew. Unfortunately for Gaston, his paternal grandmother was adopted, so he had no way to prove she wasn't Jewish. The practice of another religion, even baptism or confirmation, was not a consideration.

Lavinia was practical; she'd done her homework. She'd educated herself since she'd seen Gaston last, researching their fate like a schoolgirl. She'd made notes, assembled names of lawyers, clipped articles. Arming herself with information had helped to steady her and fill the time until she saw Gaston again. It did not prepare her however, for the way in which he wept when he told Lavinia about his imminent departure, and Céleste's accident.

Lavinia had never seen him cry with such abandon and it was deeply upsetting. He sat on her bed with his head in his hands while he talked.

"Céleste was hysterical. She was at the top of the stairs screaming as if her hair were on fire, cursing at me. It looked as if she stamped her foot and it slid out from under her. She was halfway down before her ankle got caught between two of the spindles in the stair rail."

"You mean Céleste didn't know you were Jewish?" Lavinia asked. It had never occurred to her that Céleste didn't know. Lavinia's attention had been so consumed by her concern for Gaston she hadn't even considered how it might affect Céleste.

"Céleste's leg was broken above the shin," Gaston continued. "You can't imagine what it was like on the way to the hospital." Gaston sighed and ran his hand through his hair, extending the curls with his fingers.

Céleste hadn't wanted him to leave La Rêveline, Gaston explained. All of the servants who lived on the property, in

either the main house or the attendant buildings, had left.
But for Céleste, it was deserted. Gaston took his time with
the story, weaving together the answer to Lavinia's question
with the story of the accident, building a defense on the cir-
cuitous narrative path that led to Céleste's fall.

She'd gotten the idea at Easter time, he continued, when
the gardener wrote reporting a burglary. A window had been
broken but not much had been taken, only a large copper
cauldron and some jewelry, which had almost no value now
that everyone was selling their bijoux, and nothing drove
down prices like desperation.

Whoever robbed La Rêveline had missed the point. The
cellar was still full of coal and potatoes. Enough for the winter. The barn was stacked with cords of wood; the smoke-
house had fifty pounds of seasoned game. Céleste was very
proud of that, Gaston said, and Lavinia thought, *just like a
good burgher's wife*.

Lavinia noticed that Gaston didn't mention their excellent
wine cellar; she remembered him having once described the
superior bottles he had selected over the years as compensation for spending time with his wife's family. For the first time
in more than a year, Lavinia felt the sharp fang of jealousy as
she envisioned Céleste converting the greenhouse from roses
to rutabagas, providing for Gaston, in this time of war, the
sanctuary she'd never been able to provide in marriage.

"Céleste has devoted the last decade to restoring La

Rêveline, treating it as if it were a wayward child that only she could civilize," Gaston went on, "and the house became her folly. She imagined nothing could touch us there, not even the Nazis. She became hysterical. It's even possible she fell deliberately, to keep me from leaving. When she became hysterical," he said, turning his face away from Lavinia so that she could not see his eyes, only the lines pointing to them, like a spray of arrows that have hit their mark, "I didn't know if it was because I was leaving, or Jewish, or both or neither."

In the courtyard, a bicycle bell trilled impatiently, followed by a shout from one of the de la Falaise children, calling to another, "*Hurry.*" The word swelled with import, muffling the childish laughter and sound of the entrance door slamming.

"Céleste was very young when we married," Gaston explained. "She was fresh from the nuns, and straight from the country. Her branch of the family, as I've told you, is provincial; even old Marcel Feydeau made fun of Céleste's mother, spending her fortune on hideous religious kitsch. There would have been objections to the marriage. Why should I have ruined Céleste's happiness and my own for a God I didn't worship?" he said with quiet conviction. In his hand he held a cigarette he was too distracted to light.

"It was an irrelevant complication. By the time it became relevant it was much too late. And who could have known it would come to this?" Gaston asked, his voice beginning to

crack. It was ironic, Lavinia thought, that of the three of
them, she should be the calmest. Lavinia realized too that
she'd hardened, the way even the most sensitive skin abraded
over time becomes callused.

Lavinia lifted Gaston's chin with her hand so that she
could see his face, flush and damp, hair plastered against his
forehead.

"How did you tell her, my darling? How did she learn she
was married to a Jew?" Lavinia asked. She watched his eyes
well up with tears and his chin tremble. Then Gaston started
sobbing. He let himself go for only a minute or two before he
took out a monogrammed handkerchief and blew his nose, as
if to signal the end of his tears. He stood up and began tucking in his shirt.

"You don't understand," he said. "It's complicated."

Gaston hadn't shaved and looked disheveled, even har-
rowed. Even so, Lavinia marveled at how much her body still
inclined to his, how in his presence her fingers and lips
needed to find him, despite all doubts and disappointment.
She pulled out his shirttails and ran her hand up under the
cotton fabric, feeling the rise of his chest, the warmth of his
skin and its intoxicating pull.

"Then explain it to me," she said, putting her lips to his
chin, kissing the stubble on his neck, and pushing him back
onto the unmade bed and the musty-smelling pillows.

"Take all the time in the world," Lavinia murmured,

pulling her dress over her head. An overcast sky had brought the evening early, and with it a damp chill, the hint of winter Miss Kaye always used to say lurked in autumn twilight.

"Don't be fooled," Miss Kaye had warned. "It may seem like summer during the day, but it's winter at night." Lavinia shivered closer to Gaston, pulling the covers over both of them. She had been fooled.

Gaston sang to Lavinia the next morning, making his voice quaver like Edith Piaf and hitting the high notes in an exaggerated falsetto. He was wearing Lavinia's bathrobe and he waltzed with her in the tiny kitchen. He kissed her earlobe and told her she looked radiant. The sun was striping the walls through the slats of the shutters and Gaston was even dancing with Boswell, twirling with him around the dusty room. He had never been as charming, Lavinia thought, watching Gaston smile his crooked smile as he made her an omelette.

The eggs were flecked with mushrooms from La Rêveline, and Gaston had offered them to her flamboyantly, doffing an imaginary hat and bowing low. "Nothing too dangerous or difficult," he said, "for my beloved." Gaston had brought coffee, too, which had been, with bread, among the first items rationed. "The two necessities of life," he had complained at the time, "all one really needs, in a pinch."

The previous winter the bread rationing had been a subject hard to escape. Mrs. Aiken had remarked, "Hasn't history shown us what happens when the French don't have enough bread?" It had been an especially hard privation because the harvest in 1939 had been unusually bounteous, overflowing the granaries, but so little was available to the civilians during the war that boulangeries were required to bake bread from "secondary" grains, and even then, in limited supply. When the Armistice was signed Lavinia's mailman had remarked dryly, "If they had let us eat the grain, it wouldn't have been there for the Germans. A happy thought on two counts."

"Pétain is feeding the hand that bites us," Gaston joked. "So we bite back. We will eat these eggs in honor of de Gaulle," he said, saluting her with his fork. A fleck of egg fell to the ground and Boswell trotted over to the table to scavenge.

After they finished the first pot of coffee, Lavinia made another, just as strong, using the rest of the week's supply. There was a feeling of potlatch in the air, and it felt luxurious to see the oil bead on the surface of the coffee, taste the darkness of the soil in the sweat of the bean. Gaston had also brought a bar of Belgian chocolate, which he fed her square by square, dropping them on her tongue like the host.

"Unholy wafers. Heavenly nonetheless," he said with a grin. "I know how you love extravagance," he said, "and chocolate."

They stayed in bed for hours, listening to records and holding each other. Lavinia ironed Gaston's shirt for him and then while he soaked in her bathtub, she read aloud to him from the Cocteau novel she'd recently begun. She was drunk with the pleasure of having him in her home, like playing house. He was leaving, Lavinia knew that, but not for another day.

It had taken them most of the previous day and half of the night to find an accord between their thoughts that could accommodate the accord between their bodies, and now there was so little time left Lavinia didn't want to squander any more of it.

Initially Lavinia had argued. She'd been shocked when Gaston told her of the arrangements he'd made. Her first reaction had been to exclaim, "You can't leave Céleste now!" but he had looked at her incredulously, as if it were too obvious to state.

"I can't stay!"

"But you can't just leave her like that."

"That's what you've wanted me to do all along," Gaston laughed but it was forced and laced with a bitterness that stung.

"This has nothing to do with me," she replied. "You're not leaving Céleste because of me. I'm sure you didn't even mention me." Lavinia's voice was sharper than she'd intended, and tinged with contempt. He'd presented her with a fait accompli. He had already paid for his passage.

"You needed Céleste's contacts, her money. Of course you couldn't tell her about your mistress."

"I have to leave, Lavinia. Don't make it any harder. You've seen what's happening. It will only get more difficult and dangerous to get out. This may be my last opportunity."

Their exchange had been pocked with silences in which they had listened to the wind and smoked the remainder of Gaston's tobacco. It was a harsh black flake that scalded the back of the throat but it was all that was available and therefore to be savored, like the wine they drank from the cordial glasses he had brought her as a farewell present.

They had held hands when they were not speaking. Lavinia was stunned that he had not included her in the decision, and would not be including her in the flight. It made her feel foolish, knowing she would have gone with Gaston without hesitation, no matter where he had chosen to take her. She had once written to him,

My darling,
I want to see you shave, sleep, cry, vomit. I want
to be the one who wipes fever from your brow. I want
to be the only one your heart tutoyers.

Even now, having seen Gaston degrade himself with lies and deceptions, parlaying selfishness into heroism, even now, she knew if he took her by the hand he could lead her into a burning building. He would send word as soon as he was safe. He would send word from Switzerland. Gaston had repeated it with conviction and kisses. It would be easier to arrange their future from there, he'd said, but Lavinia wondered with a sickening flutter in her stomach if that wasn't something he'd also told Céleste.

In the courtyard, Madame Braun's loose shutter knocked against the wall whenever the wind shifted direction. The hinge had a particularly plaintive song; it reminded Lavinia of the interrogative lilt in a bobwhite's call, and the disquieting resonance of an unanswered question.

"I have no choice."

"I know."

Gaston gave her a silver bracelet and a key, and asked of her one small favor.

"The silver bracelet was my mother's. It's the only thing of hers I have and I want you to have it. The cordial glasses I gave you may be more valuable, but I hope you'll treasure this as well. I should have given it to you sooner. I should have given you all manner of jewelry. I'm sorry."

"Hush," Lavinia said, kissing him. "It's very beautiful. Now tell me what favor you intend to exact in exchange. Odds are pretty good you'll get it, and I don't even know what it is."

Gaston laughed. It was the first deep laugh she'd heard in a while and she watched him surrender to it, letting his head tip back and his shoulders rise as it rolled through his body, like a wave sweeping him up.

"I'm glad I haven't turned your head with my baubles," he said dryly. Gaston took her hand and spread it open. "This key," he said, placing it in the center of her palm and then closing her hand around it, "was Marcel Feydeau's." His tone shifted, and his levity was gone.

"It opens a storage room at 34, Rue Vaneau, filled with boxes of paperwork from his years in law. I forgot about it. The concierge forgot about it too. I found the key a few months ago in my desk when I was looking for documents having to do with my mother. I want you to go through the files and papers and see if you can find Marcel's diaries. Feydeau kept them in ledger books. Marcel gave me the key before he died and asked me to promise to destroy them. He was the only one of Céleste's relatives I genuinely liked. He was good to me and I owe it to him. I feel as if it would be bad luck not to do it.

"I was planning to do it this week but my departure date changed. I was told I had only this weekend, so I decided to spend the time with you. I didn't want to waste it in a musty cellar tying up loose ends."

Gaston put his arms around her waist and held her, swaying ever so slightly as he tightened his hug.

"I knew I could count on you," he said, resting his chin on the top of her head. "And you know, Marcel Feydeau represented some distinguished names in his day. You may find letters from someone famous, or better still, infamous. Something to reward your effort. Take whatever is of interest or value, and burn the diaries." There was an ominous finality in the gesture, but Lavinia nodded, "Of course.

Gaston was secretive about his contact, and sketchy about his route, revealing only that he changed "escort" twice along the way and that it was fabulously expensive. As the time of Gaston's departure drew closer, he became restless, and distracted. It was hard to know what to do with the little time they had left, but any more time than they had would have made it impossible for her to choke back her grief, to remain practical, equal to the moment.

They played a halfhearted game of cards and Gaston repacked his suitcase twice. The first time he removed an extra bar of soap and a Portuguese dictionary. The second time, he withdrew a volume of Montaigne's essays and a pair of black leather wing tips.

"Here," he said, handing her the book, "take this. I don't want you to get bored without me." Then he handed her the shoes: "These are for Boswell, so that he doesn't get bored without me either." She laughed and so did Gaston, forgetting momentarily the suffocating circumstances. Lavinia opened the book randomly and read aloud, "One should always have one's boots on and be ready to leave."

"Brilliant," Lavinia said, closing the book. "I can't wait to take my boots off and dig in."

His optimism seemed to erode as the afternoon lengthened and rain clouds gathered again behind the dome of the Panthéon. Gaston commented irritably on the weather, and the shutter that wouldn't stop banging in the wind. He tightened the laces of his shoes and asked for a tisane, which he didn't drink. When Gaston complained about the way Boswell drooled in his sleep, Lavinia stood behind Gaston with her head on his back, her arms tight around his waist. She pressed herself against him like that until she could feel his shoulders begin to relax, and his breath deepen.

He turned around and held her face, stroking her hair, kissing her forehead. "It will all work out. You'll see. I'll be fine." It seemed to calm him to reassure her, and he sounded convinced again.

"Céleste will be fine, too. The doctor told me himself. He said she was very lucky with the way the bone broke. So you see," Gaston concluded, "she'll mend in no time. It's just a quesition of bed rest. And I've made the necessary arrangements for that."

Previously, Céleste had been portrayed as sickly, suffering from a host of ailments both real and imagined. Resilience was not an attribute Lavinia associated with Céleste, who learned nonetheless to wield her frailty like a weapon and would punish Gaston by throwing her back out, or taking to bed, incapacitating herself just enough to command attention and concern. Lavinia understood, however, from Gaston's anxious rationalizations, that the degree to which he insisted Céleste's health was not in doubt was the degree to which, this time, it was. "I've made arrangements," he repeated several times, "Céleste will get better care than I could give her."

At quarter to five, Gaston stood and smiled. It was a quick, nervous flutter on his lips that resolved into an almost imperceptible sigh. He put on his coat. As he readied himself to leave, adjusting his scarf, Lavinia felt the room become charged with an adrenal energy that was both exhilarating and sickening and bordered on hysteria. She walked with Gaston to the subway, holding his arm tightly, trying to stay in step with him, trying to keep her body as close to his as possible without breaking stride. Gaston had asked her not to enter the station. He was supposed to be alone when the contact approached him.

It was just as well, Lavinia thought, not to have a tearful farewell on the platform. Instead, Lavinia tried to memorize every detail, as if they were grains of sand slipping away: the pale glow of cobblestones in the sunlight, a doorbell's nasal buzz, the flap of wings stirring up the air overhead, the peeling red *R* in a Ricard advertisement painting on the side of a building and the feel of his wool coat against her wrist. It was almost a relief when he finally walked out of view, descending into the Métro station with a quick backward glance, mouthing the words *Je t'adore.*

Lavinia listened to the lurch of traffic as the lights changed, the whistle of a man calling his dog back to him. It seemed impossible that everything should go on as normal. Lavinia walked a block and a half before she began to cry. Then, she squatted in the doorway of a shop that had closed, and let herself howl. It didn't matter that the hem of her coat was getting soiled and that people were staring, or that she didn't have a handkerchief with her. When she finally got home, her eyes were swollen into slits and her throat was raw.

"I love you, Lavinia," Gaston had said at the Métro. "You taught me how."

His chin was scraped from shaving with a dull blade, and his hair, just a little too long, was tousled out of place by the wind into a boyish disorder. Something about his posture, the hunch of his shoulders, reminded her of Grisette, the scrappy cat from the Rue Vaneau.

"Don't worry, Lavinia. It will work out," Gaston said one final time, rubbing her cheek with the back of his finger, "for all of us: Céleste will have Delphine and Jean-Marc at La Rêveline, taking care of her, and you and I will have snow, and chocolate, and each other." He looked back just once, mouthing his last message to her as the crowd from an arriving train pushed past him up the stairs.

When Lavinia got home, she had not even gotten her coat off, her key was still in her hand when she realized what Gaston had said. *He didn't know.* It was a staggering thought: Gaston didn't know Jean-Marc was dead, that he'd passed out drunk, and choked on his own vomit. Delphine had found him curled up under the kitchen table, wearing a gas mask, clutching a polished pair of shoes. It had happened while Gaston was still out of town, at La Rêveline.

When Jean-Marc hadn't shown up at any of his neighborhood spots for several days running, Lavinia had made inquiries.

"It was too much for the poor woman," a neighbor said, "after all that she's endured, finding him like that." The concierge said Delphine had gone to be with her brother. She'd left no address. "I've a bundle of mail I don't know what to do with, and she still owes last month's rent. We all have our own sad stories, but one still has to pay the rent," the concierge complained before closing her window.

Now that Gaston was gone, Lavinia was the only one who knew that Céleste was alone at La Rêveline, imprisoned in bed by her plaster cast. Lavinia had no idea of how to contact Céleste's family or even if her mother would be disposed to care for a daughter whose marriage she claimed no longer to recognize, who had been made impure by twenty years of cohabitation with a Jew.

Lavinia had no other choice but to go to La Rêveline, even though it was the very last place she wished to go. In a vacuum, Céleste became her responsibility. "Knowledge is a burden," she told Madame Luberon, when she explained why she needed a counterfeit Permis de Circulation Temporaire and a new *carte d'identité*. She had turned to Madame Luberon because she had not known what else to do, and because, oddly enough, Lavinia trusted her.

"I know you hate the Jews, and the rich, and Americans, and Bolsheviks, and me," Lavinia had said to Madame Luberon, "but I am counting on your hating Nazis most of all. If you can't help me, tell me who can."

It was precisely Madame Luberon's lack of sentiment that enabled Lavinia to read her more accurately than some of their more conflicted neighbors. Madame Luberon regarded Lavinia, considering the question, her arms crossed in front of her heavy bosom.

"My husband is dead," she spat out. "His brother is dead. Don't make trouble for yourself. Myself, I'm staying out of its way. There are bullets in the wall of number 79, down the block, where Pierre Ponceau, the butcher's son, got in its way. Have a look."

"Please," Lavinia said, "I don't know what else to do. I wish I didn't know about her being trapped there, but I do, so it's up to me. I have to go. There's no one else to do it. It's been two days already." Her heart was beating wildly in her chest, and she wondered if Madame Luberon had in fact been the one who reported Madame Braun's sister to the authorities.

"Don't know what to do? That must be a first for you," Madame Luberon sneered. She lit the stub of a cigarette that still had a puff or two left in it and shook her head. Boswell yawned, sneezed twice, shook himself, and sneezed again. Lavinia picked him up and held him to her chest like a baby. One of his eyes was getting clouded and he had developed a bald patch on his ear. He licked her chin and sneezed again. Lavinia had already turned and started to walk away when Madame Luberon croaked out, "Come back in five hours. And I'll need three copies of the same photograph as soon as possible."

As Madame Luberon shuffled away in her bedroom slippers, her husband's coat hanging bulkily from her shoulders, she added with an air of authority, "Take rice and sugar and salt. Those are the staples she'll most need to supplement a kitchen garden."

Madame Luberon had a cigarette jutting from the corner of her mouth, her eyes squinting away the smoke, as she later pasted Lavinia's photograph into a coupon book with a French name and an address in the same district as La Rêveline.

"You didn't ask for this," Madame Luberon said, pointing to a Carte d'Alimentation Individuelle, "but I threw it in for you anyway, because of the little dog. If you don't have one with the same address as the *carte d'identité* it will look suspicious. Besides, you may need to eat." Madame Luberon laughed harshly, letting a long head of ash fall from her cigarette. Then she coughed, a long phlegmy struggle for breath that left her slightly winded.

"I'll keep the dog for you," Madame Luberon said casually. Lavinia was surprised and touched by the offer. It brought to her eyes the tears she had refused to let Madame Luberon elicit in the past.

"Thank you," Lavinia said. "I couldn't bear to leave Boswell behind, but thank you."

Madame Luberon shrugged. "I didn't think so," she said and then she turned away, and lumbered off, without saying good-bye.

"Your French is an abomination," she added, as she walked away. "Wrap your throat with camphor-coated rags, and avoid any unnecessary talk along the way. Enough camphor so that you really stink, and then only whisper."

"What else?"

"Pray," Madame Luberon said, letting her door swing closed behind her with a thud that rattled its glass panel.

When Lavinia set off with Boswell and a small leather satchel, she wasn't afraid, although she knew she should be. The moisture from all the recent rain made the air seem colder, and the horizon farther. The trip felt like an unfair obligation thrust upon her like Service du Travail Obligatoire. Lavinia had included in her luggage a copy of *Madame Bovary,* a book selected for spite.

Lavinia had no way of knowing that she would be at La Rêveline for much longer than a weekend. It hadn't occurred to her that Céleste might have had a stroke by the time she got there, or that by caring for her, Lavinia would become invested with the same irrational love with which she might have tended a baby bird, but with a more profound implication.

Lavinia couldn't foresee the way she would laugh with Céleste, or share confidences. She never imagined, as she walked away from Paris and farther from Gaston, in two pairs of socks and old hiking boots, that there would be no easy replacement to whom she could delegate the unlikely role that circumstance imposed, or that in caring *for* Céleste she would come to care *about* her with an increasingly fierce tenderness as Céleste's health declined, and they abandoned all reserve with which they talked together.

Tucked within the pages of the book was one of the first letters Gaston had sent her, the only one from that time that had escaped her purge. When she'd found it, Lavinia read it over and over again, investing it with the power of a talisman, the significance of a sign. Just seeing Gaston's handwriting had flooded her with emotions that clarified and complicated the situation.

Mademoiselle Gibbs,

I, who thought I knew so much about love, am in terra incognita, a landscape more wild and lovely than any I've walked before. Last night I wandered home along the Seine and marveled at my happiness. For a moment near the Pont Neuf, I was overwhelmed: tears came to my eyes and my throat felt like it was parched. It was not just the relief of an answered prayer. It was awe for a bounty that so exceeded my imaginings that I could not measure in words what my heart felt.

It made Lavinia feel both beautiful and bereft. It made her realize the fullness of her humanity, and the price of love; that even if she had been raised by wolves, she was not one of them. In the end, that was enough to be true to, alone on the darkling plain.

Acknowledgments

I am deeply grateful to Marjorie Braman, who was magnificently patient and undoubting. I would also like to thank Jamie Bernstein, Jody Caravaglia, Anne Cherry, Miriam Clark, Bill Clegg, Anne Griffin, Lisa Gilbert, Beth McFadden, Dan Medcalf, Tom Rauffenbart, Helen Simonson, Gerry Wallman, and Matty Ward for cheering me on when I needed it most, and Andrea Barnet for the use of her studio. I also want to thank Kathy Robbins, and my mother for her support in the darkest hours. Aso Tavitian deserves so much thanks he gets his own sentence. I am indebted to all those who championed this book in any number of ways.